PEACE PULAO

PEACE PULAO

VIBHA BATRA

HarperCollins *Children's Books*

First published in India by HarperCollins *Children's* Books 2025
An imprint of HarperCollins *Publishers*
HarperCollins *Publishers* India, Cyber City,
Building 10-A, Gurugram, Haryana-122002, India
www.harpercollins.co.in

2 4 6 8 10 9 7 5 3 1

P-ISBN: 978-93-6989-240-2
E-ISBN: 978-93-6989-817-6

Typeset in 12/16.3 Scala Sans Pro
by HarperCollins *Publishers* India Pvt. Ltd

Printed and bound at
Thomson Press (India) Ltd

MIX
Paper | Supporting responsible forestry
FSC® C010615

This book is produced from independently certified FSC® paper to ensure responsible forest management.

HarperCollins Publishers, Macken House, 39/40 Mayor Street Upper, Dublin 1, D01 C9W8, Ireland

For NBMPRS

Contents

1

The Bread Always Falls on the Buttered Side

IT WAS A SCORCHING, SWELTERING, sizzling morning. The oldest bazaar of Pasinabad was teeming with true-blue foodies, thrifty shopaholics, cawing crows, cowy cows, speeding cyclists, screeching cycle rickshaws, pushy push-cart vendors and pained pedestrians. Oh, and tireless tourists. A record number of tourists. During peak season, they outnumbered the locals. After all, Pasinabad was renowned for its courtly manners, crumbling monuments, chikankari masterpieces and culinary marvels.

'Dum Biryani! Yum Biryani! Welcome, Biryani!' shouted human signboards stationed outside restaurants, in an attempt to tempt passers-by. An invitation that was followed by lightning-fast hands grabbing and dragging the unsuspecting pedestrians into the eateries. In fact, it wasn't uncommon to see a selfie-happy tourist stop by to ask for directions, only to be bundled inside and plonked at a table, to emerge an hour later with a bursting belly, a doggy bag and a bill longer than a fully unfurled toilet roll.

Suraiya had parked herself outside Shaan-e-Daawat for precisely this reason. There she was, looking prim and proper in a Peter-Pan collar dress and ballet flats. Her silky hair held back by a padded velvet headband, bangs sweeping across her forehead. Firm jaw, piercing gaze. All of eleven. Brisk and business-like, she was set to 'invite' customers into her Dada Jaan's restaurant. It was how things were done in Pasinabad. The town was like no other. It was founded by Nawab Naak-Mein-Dum, after all.

It's a scientific fact that historians barely see eye-to-eye on anything, and yet, it was widely accepted in historical circles that Nawab Naak-Mein-Dum was a Royal Pain-in-the-Bum. That he was useless, senseless, and good-for-nothing. That turning Pasinabad into the food capital of the country was the first and last sensible thing His Hopeless Highness had ever done. Not surprisingly, the town still tingled with tales of his lavish feasts, lazy habits and loony ideas. Ideas such as:

- naming the town after a bodily function (perspiration, of all things!)
- banning eyebrows from the kingdom ("Eyebrows? Who needs eyebrows!")
- refusing to sit on a throne (preferring to perch His Royal Bottom on a giant pumpkin or watermelon or jackfruit instead)

Speaking of loony ideas, Suraiya felt one bubbling up in her head as she spotted someone. Straw hat. Cargo shorts.

Black backpack. White sneakers. Fancy camera. Mineral water. Aha! Foreign tourist! She got ready to dangle an irresistible bait to reel him in. Lifting a hand like an elephant's trunk, she was about to trumpet loudly, when...

TEHREHREHREHREHREHREHREH! A snake charmer's been began playing out of nowhere.

The enticing bait! Someone had beaten her to it!

Suraiya swung sharply to the left. A boy, around the same age as her, stood there, bursting with energy and barely contained excitement. In a red-checked shirt worn over a plain white tee and khaki shorts, he was all bouncy curls and deep dimples, moon face and puppy-dog eyes brimming with enthusiasm.

Divumber. Next door neighbour. Arch rival. Sworn enemy. He'd landed up in Pasinabad around the same time as her and stationed himself outside Awadh Mahal to usher customers into his granny's restaurant. And *this* is what he'd been doing ever since! Pulling all sorts of stunts, luring away customers, stealing Shaan-e-Daawat's business.

Suraiya was momentarily mesmerized as Divumber played an imaginary been. With a loud hiss, he held his hands above his head like a hooded cobra.

The tourist was a goner from the word go. He stopped dead in his tracks, hypnotized.

'This way, Ssssss-sir!' Divumber swayed, before wriggling on the ground in a most undignified Nagin Dance.

Suraiya watched as her dollars danced to Divumber's tune.

'Real In-di-ah,' the tourist breathed, before dashing her hopes and dashing inside enemy territory.

'You...*snake*,' Suraiya spluttered like cumin seeds in oil.

Divumber flashed her a reptilian grin before slithering inside Awadh Mahal.

Suraiya blew her bangs out of her face. 'Wait till our fancy new menu cards arrive,' she challenged his receding back. Where *were* they, she wondered, standing on tiptoes to stare out into the street.

A willowy young woman bustled over. She was wearing a hairnet, a dazed smile and the dreamy expression of someone who's just tasted a delish new dish.

'What's taking the menus so long, Roshanara?' Suraiya frowned at her distant cousin and Shaan-e-Daawat's Head Bawarchi.

'Don't worry, Su. I've spoken to the printers. They'll be here any minute now.'

Suraiya rubbed her palms gleefully. She'd picked a rich blue and gold colour palette (hello, everyone knows it's the colour of royalty!), googled stylish logo options, downloaded lip-smacking food photos and created quirky doodles to spice up the design. Even the graphic designer had been impressed.

Alas! The customers arrived before the new menu cards could.

Which is why the minute the delivery boy landed up, Suraiya plucked the parcel from his hand, ripped open the packaging and barrelled inside, abandoning her post at the entrance. She'd driven herself nuts, imagining the worst: Customers demanding the menu, drumming their fingers impatiently on the table, checking their watches, before leaving their menu-less restaurant in a huff and heading over to Awadh Mahal.

'Shouldn't we go through them once?' murmured Roshanara, tailing Suraiya as she hopped from table to table, distributing the menu cards.

'No time,' mumbled Suraiya as she handed it to a family of ten.

She was patting herself on the back for placing the menus in record time, when she heard giggles, followed by loud guffaws from the table next to her, and then, shrieks of laughter from the table in the corner. Before she knew it, everyone was cackling, and clicking pictures of the menu cards.

'What's going on?' whispered Roshanara in alarm.

Suraiya dashed to the closest table and flashed a smile. 'Hell...'

The 'o' got stuck in her throat as her eyes fell on the menu card, the one she'd designed so painstakingly.

- **Pasina Pulao**
- **Paneer Paw-sand**
- **Almond Chee-ra**
- **Goondi Raita**
- **Nargisi Kurta**
- **Kutta Curry**
- **Ganji ke Vade**
- **Malala Kofta**
- **Kachcha Parantha**
- **Hathi Kebab**
- **Beti Parantha**
- **Tan Pulao**
- **Button Mushroom**
- **Yak Pulao**
- **Pain Naan**

On and on it went. All of the dishes misspelt, with mentions of elephants and underwear and whatnot.

Suraiya staggered back in shock. She'd checked the handwritten menu. Proofread it. Several times. So had Roshanara. They'd made sure everything was A-okay before hand-delivering it to the printers. How had things gone so horribly, horridly, horrifically wrong? HOW?

'This is a crime!' Suraiya cried out.

The words were barely out of her mouth when a brawny policewoman sprang up from a table like a mountain goat between rocks. 'Crime? Report the crime! The name is Bul. Chul-bul. Have no fear, Inspector Chulbul is here.'

Suraiya flew to her. 'Sorry, sorry. False alarm.'

The cop's eyes darted around the restaurant. 'This beauty is always on duty. Mind it!'

Suraiya was still soothing the seething cop when Dada Jaan bobbed into the scene, like a boat in choppy seas. 'Adab!' he greeted a family, ambling up to their table. 'All okay?' He looked at the grinning faces of the patrons. 'Everyone seems to be having fun.'

'At our expense,' muttered Suraiya. Tucking a menu card under her arm, she tugged at DJ's arm, leading him away.

'What happened?' asked DJ when they reached the reception area.

Suraiya handed him the menu card wordlessly. One look at the misspelt words running across the page like mischievous monkeys, and DJ sat down heavily on the diwan. 'What about the old menus?'

Suraiya went pink. 'I, um, tossed them in the dumpster earlier this morning. Bad idea, I see that now.'

DJ let out a groan.

They sat in silence as Roshanara exchanged heated words (softly) with someone on the phone a little distance away. 'The printer says they printed exactly what they'd received,' she updated.

After much questioning, cross-questioning and finger-pointing, they realized there was nothing to be done. They were stuck with these menus.

Suraiya's heart-shaped face clouded. 'I feel like it's my fault.'

'That's because it is,' said Roshanara helpfully. 'New menu cards. Your bright idea.'

Suraiya's shoulders drooped. 'Sorry, DJ.'

'You were only trying to help.' DJ patted her head gently. 'What's done is done. From now on, let's be very very careful, okay?' he said, stretching the syllables like chewing gum. 'It's that time of year. When Machli Star Inspectors start visiting all the Pasinabad restaurants!'

2

A Fine Kettle of Fish

SURAIYA KNIT HER EYEBROWS. 'THE what?'

'Every year, the Machli Committee awards stars of excellence to the best restaurants in town,' explained DJ. 'They send out a team of food experts to inspect restaurants around Pasinabad.'

'The identity of these experts is the biggest secret in town,' added Roshanara. 'They come in disguise—dressed like commonfolk, order their meals, pay for them and leave as quietly as they'd arrived.'

'Like ordinary customers? Why?'

'To make sure no one makes a fuss over them,' explained Roshanara. 'To make sure no one gives them bribes or special treatment. That way they can judge and rate us impartially.'

Makes sense, mused Suraiya.

'The winning restaurants are awarded a shining Machli Star. *And* they are listed on the prestigious Machli Guide Books.' A sheepish smile came over DJ's face. 'We've been trying to bag a Machli Star for a while now. Quite unsuccessfully, I must confess.'

An idea whizzed into Suraiya's brain. If they could bag a Machli Star, it'd solve all their problems! It'd put Shaan-e-Daawat on the map. On the front page of *Petu Times*. On every 'Top 10 Restaurants' list. And once that happened, they'd never have to worry again. Foodies would come from all over—Pasinabad, India, abroad—like bees to honey, like monkeys to bananas, like influencers to Instagram. Who knew, perhaps one day there'd be no need to 'usher' customers into the restaurant. If they got enough paying customers, they'd get influencers, reviews, media, publicity. *Free*. They'd never have to compete with Awadh Mahal again. They'd leave it far, far behind. In the dust. Where it belonged.

Suraiya put her warrior face on. She'd make sure the Machli Star Inspector went home impressed. She'd make sure Shaan-e-Daawat bagged a Machli Star. She'd make sure everything—every. little. thing.—was perfect.

'We'll order another set of menu cards,' DJ's voice interrupted her daydream. 'No harm done.'

Harm. Suraiya's brain snagged on the word. What if someone was out to *harm* Shaan-e-Daawat? What if the menu accident wasn't an accident? What if it was *sabotage*? Suraiya's head spun. Who'd do such a thing? Who'd stoop so low? Who'd sink to such depths? She gasped. Someone who had a bone to pick with them. Someone like their next-door neighbour! She wanted to go barging into their restaurant and tell them she was on to them. If only she had some evidence of wrongdoing. She straightened her shoulders. Well, if proof was needed, proof she'd get. They'd messed with the wrong girl.

***

'This is wrong, wrong, *wrong*!' Divumber squawked in horror next door. He gaped at the strapping young man next to him.

'Nononooo!' moaned Gajodhar, the Head Bawarchi of Awadh Mahal.

They were in the pantry, staring at the new signboard. The signage company had only just delivered it. Luckily, at the back door, so as not to inconvenience the customers. They'd be back at night to install it. The signboard was just as they'd promised: lightweight, durable, bright.

It was also a disaster.

AWFUL MAHAL—it screamed in awfully gigantic, cheery, shouty capitals.

Divumber had chosen a traffic-stopping letter size, an ornate font and a deep, velvety purple background (it was the colour of royalty, after all). Unable to wait till closing time to see his creativity come to life, he'd ripped open the newspaper-brown tape packaging, trembling with excitement.

And now, he was still trembling. For an altogether different reason.

'Mataji's going to have my head for it.' Gajodhar clutched his head. 'What are we going to do now?'

'Call the signboard company,' wailed Divumber. He desperately tried to erase the AWFUL with his spit. In vain.

'Already did. They said it's not their fault. In fact, they accused *us* of giving them the wrong spelling,' groaned the Head Bawarchi. 'I've already made the full payment.'

'Let's hide it!' Divumber looked around him wildly.

'But how long can our restaurant go without a signboard?' screeched Gajodhar. 'What'll we tell Mataji?'

'Tell me what?'

'Mataji!' Divumber spun around and came face to face with his granny.

Draped in a pastel pink chikankari saree with shimmery sequins and colourful tassels, a delicate strand of pearls gracing her neck, and her hair styled in a fashionable bob, Mataji looked like a modern Maharani. She was holding a gold-plated walking cane in one hand and a platter of leftovers in the other.

As her eyes fell on the signboard, her rimless spectacles nearly misted up in shock.

Gajodhar quickly took the platter of leftovers from her hand before it fell down with a deafening *thunkkk*.

'I shouldn't have tried to change things around, Mataji,' Divumber said in a small voice. 'The old signboard was great. This was an awful...', he squirmed, 'erm, bad idea.'

'There are no bad ideas, just bad times.' Mataji sighed so deeply that for a moment Divumber was worried she'd exhaled all the air from her lungs.

'I thought you'd be mad when you found out.'

Mataji ruffled his hair. 'Thanks to the meditation classes, I've found inner peace.'

Divumber looked at her closely. She spent all her afternoons learning deep breathing techniques. And from the looks of it, the course had worked wonders. His hot-tempered, short-tempered granny was now radiating peace and calm.

'Why don't you put your afternoons to good use, too?' Mataji advised, as Gajodhar laid out the leftovers on the gully wall for birds, ants, insects and the neighbourhood cats. 'Why don't you sign up for a summer course? Didn't you say you wanted to learn—'

'Why go anywhere when there's an expert at home?' Divumber cut in. 'Why can't *you* teach me?'

Mataji was smiling at him when her eyes fell on the newspaper the signboard had come wrapped in. It was the front page of *Petu Times*. She reached for it, frowning. Divumber scooped it up and handed it to her.

Her frown deepened as she skimmed through the paper.

'KAMBAKHT!' she exploded, scaring off the crows that were enjoying the leftovers. 'May they take a giant bite of a kebab only to realise they're wearing someone's dentures! May they spill Jal-Jeera on their lap so everyone thinks it's susu! May the waistbands of all their underwear be stretchier than seviyaan!' She glared at the supplement, before squashing it like a malai kofta and flinging it away.

Divumber sighed. So much for inner peace.

Still, he knew if Mataji was dishing out creative curses, it could only mean one thing: awful news. Divumber picked up the paper ball and uncrumpled it.

AWADH MAHAL – AN OLD-WORLD RELIC, blared the headline of the food review column.

Divumber proceeded to read it out loud in a posh TV announcer voice: 'The once-upon-a-time grand restaurant is now a shadow of its former self. The flaking paint, the fading purple décor, the low seating with off-white mattresses set against the wall with matching bolsters, the gilded mirrors, the Nawab's paintings, the fragrance of rose attar lingering in the air, the chandeliers with several bulbs missing . . . all spell haunted ruins. With a Miss Havisham presiding over it.

And then there are the rules. So many rules. People go out for a meal to have fun, not to follow rules!

If you're from the last century, this might just be the place for you. But in case you were born *after* India got its independence, make a beeline for another restaurant. Luckily, Pasinabad's crawling with them!'

DÉCOR: ★
FOOD: ★★★
SERVICE: ★★
OVERALL EXPERIENCE: ★

3

The Apple Doesn't Fall Far from the Tree

'WHO'S MISS HAVISHAM?' DIVUMBER ASKED no one in particular. He looked up from the paper to find Mataji and Gajodhar glaring at him. 'I mean, what a nasty review!'

Things had taken a rotten turn indeed.

Divumber hated to admit it, but the reviewer had a point. Awadh Mahal *did* look ancient. It *was* falling apart. And it *was* frequented by people who were born in the 1800s. As for The Rules, shudder!

MATAJI'S RULES

1. **No forks, no spoons. (Food's best enjoyed without cutlery.)**
2. **No menus.**
3. **No special requests.**
4. **No selfies (Self before selfie. It isn't just a meal. It's an experience to be enjoyed. With all your senses.)**

5. **No reservations. Walk-ins only.**
6. **No requests for chairs.**
7. **No requests for Western music.**
8. **No requests for fusion dishes.**
9. **No, you cannot speak to the *chef* (we don't have one. We do have a highly trained Head Bawarchi whose job is to cook, not to meet and greet guests).**
10. **Those asking for discount will be charged 10% extra.**
11. **So will paan-spitters.**
12. **Leave your attitude outside.**
13. **Badly behaved patrons will be shown the door.**
14. **Put your phones and babies on silent mode.**
15. **Just joking. Babies not allowed.**

Divumber's moon face clouded. Was the reviewer right? Was the restaurant too fuddy-duddy? Was it losing out on popularity, patrons and promising five-star ratings because of Mataji's old-fashioned approach? The thought went round and round his head.

'Some people! Can't tell kheer from phirni, but want to do restaurant reviews. Bah!' Mataji fumed.

'Who people?'

'Don't you know?' Gajodhar snapped. 'Those selfie-stick-wielding so-called food influencers, who turn up at restaurants and demand a free meal in exchange for an honest review.'

Divumber faked an outburst of coughs. 'Oh, you mean the Freeloader Mafia? I knew that.' He could imagine Mataji's reaction. She would've turned them down faster than a TV on full volume. And now, she was paying the price of refusing them. Who knew turning down a free review request could prove to be so expensive?

'This is a personal attack,' bristled the Head Bawarchi.

Divumber felt a pang. Awadh Mahal was his granny's whole life. She'd worked tirelessly to make the restaurant what it was: Pasinabad's Pulao Paradise. She'd spent years and years perfecting the family recipes that had been handed down over the generations.

'Don't worry, Mataji,' he said consolingly, 'no one reads food reviews these days.'

'Really?' Mataji asked hopefully.

Divumber bobbed his head.

'Really?' asked Gajodhar, when Mataji turned around.

Divumber shook his head.

'Off to meditation class,' Mataji announced glumly.

'Really?' Divumber yelped incredulously, then hastily changed it to, 'I mean, clearly, it's working.'

Mataji shuffled away, Gajodhar at her heels.

Divumber leaned against the wall. He wondered if the Head Bawarchi was right. Was it a personal attack? He snatched up the newspaper and stared at the reviewer's name till he saw spots behind his eyes. Who was this 'Foodie ka Funda'? Chef? Foodie? Influencer? Someone with a bone to pick with Mataji? Divumber gasped as a thought popped up in his mind. Someone like their next-door neighbour? Wasn't she always playing a game of 'Better Than You'? Wasn't she always blowing her own shehnai? And what had she said last week? 'You're going down down down, Mister!'

Trash Awadh Mahal in print and steal their customers away—was that her sinister plan?

***

'ARRRRRGHHHHHHH!' Suraiya shared her frustration with the empty restaurant as she scribbled furiously in her glittery notebook.

Like all other establishments in Pasinabad, Shaan-e-Daawat was closed between lunch and dinner, giving them a few hours of respite, before the mad rush began all over again. But instead of chilling on the comfy diwan in the reception area, she was bristling at the way things had turned out that morning.

'And I'm back!' Roshanara said, gliding into the restaurant. 'Hope you didn't miss me, but—'

'But you *really* needed some fresh air,' Suraiya snorted. She was used to Roshanara's daily disappearance.

'Oh-ho! Bad mood?' The Head Bawarchi flopped down next to her. 'Still thinking about the menu cards?' Suraiya shook her head.

'Oh! What did that'—Roshanara looked around furtively—Burnt Brinjal do now?'

She meant Divumber & Family aka They-Who-Must-Not-Be-Named. Talking about them was strictly forbidden inside the restaurant. And even though Dada Jaan was napping at home, safely tucked into bed like a napkin into a collar, the Head Chef wasn't taking any chances.

Suraiya narrated the snake charmer story. 'I'd almost grabbed the tourist,' she hissed. 'If that Bitter Broccoli hadn't made an utter fool of himself...Nagin Dance! In the middle of the street. Ewwww! Who does that?' Scorn dripped from her voice, but deep inside she couldn't help but feel a smidge of envy at the underhanded tactic. *Why didn't I think of it*, she berated herself. *Should've known the tourist would lap it up.*

'Such a Smarty Samosa he is,' said Roshanara with grudging admiration, reclining against the throw cushions.

'Hey! Whose side are you on?' Suraiya glared at her. 'Praising the enemy!'

'Enemy? That's a bit much, na?'

'Didn't you say the families have been feuding for ages? That DJ hasn't spoken to the neighbours since forever? What does that make us?' Suraiya held up a hand. 'Don't say "competition", okay?'

Roshanara closed her mouth, wishing she'd kept her mouth shut when Suraiya had first arrived in Pasinabad, around two weeks ago. But no, she'd proceeded to share an in-depth report of the rivalry.

As it happened, people took food very seriously in Pasinabad. And the food business was a full-on competitive sport. There were more restaurants in town than people. BUT. Only two served the iconic Pasinabad Pulao, as opposed to the generic biryani. Shaan-e-Daawat and Awadh Mahal. It didn't help that the two rivals were joined at the hip, like a perpetually bickering pair of conjoined twins. As if a clueless chef had tossed two potentially explosive ingredients in a pan and squished, squashed, squooshed them together.

'Shaan-e-Daawat is Pasinabad's bestest, finest, greatest, highest, toppest...' Suraiya ran out of adjectives, but not out of steam. 'See?' She jerked a thumb at the proof. Oh, not at the heavy digital safe in which Dada Jaan deposited the cash, but at the bronze plaque nestled against a red velvet pillow in a glass case. The historical artifact was mounted atop a wooden pedestal and proudly displayed in the reception area. **Rakabdar to Nawab Naak-Mein-Dum,** the inscription declared in Urdu.

'The Nawab granted the title and honour of Personal Chef to *my* great-great-great grandfather—Ustad Aflatoon. A gourmet cook, a boy genius with a taste for adventure, who revolutionized the dining experience with his food innovations,' Suraiya said, loftily. 'Shaan-e-Daawat has a historic connection to Pasinabad.'

'So does Awadh Mahal,' Roshanara reminded her. '*Their* ancestor—Ustad Ajeebogareeb—was a Rakabdar too, and he also received a plaque.'

Suraiya scoffed. Deep inside, though, she was super worried. Things were heating up on the rivalry front. Which is why she'd spent the entire afternoon drawing up a list of ideas to:

1. Crack the menu mystery
2. Attract more customers

The menu was a taunt; the Nagin Dance was a dare. Suraiya squared her shoulders. Challenge accepted. She'd plant the victory flag on every Pasinabadi Petu's plate. She'd win their hearts, minds and tummies. She'd take Shaan-e-Daawat to dizzying heights. 'That Pulpy Papaya better run—'

'Suraiya, meri jaan.' Dada Jaan rustled into the restaurant like a summer breeze.

'DJ!' Suraiya's face turned red.

Caught! Red-handed! Talking about the enemy!

4

Take It With a Pinch of Salt

'KYA KHICHDI PAK RAHI HAI?' DJ asked suspiciously, looking from Suraiya to Roshanara. 'What mischief are you up to?'

'Coming!' Roshanara called out to an imaginary person, scurrying away to the kitchen.

'We were...uh...just thinking up ways to nab more customers, DJ.'

'Hmm.' Dada Jaan plonked down on the gadda.

'Looking sharp,' Suraiya commented.

DJ was always perfectly turned out. On a typical workday, he looked dapper. Today, he was in a pristine white kurta-pyjama, a maroon waistcoat with delicate zardozi embroidery, a matching velvet cap and handcrafted jootis with upturned soles.

'Always! How do you think I get voted Best Dressed Guest at the Machli Gala year after year?' He produced a crinkly supari pouch from his kurta pocket, tore it open rather messily and emptied the contents directly into his mouth.

Suraiya goggled. 'First, Machli Star. Now Machli Gala. Two two?'

'A pair of fish is our state's emblem, after all.' DJ chewed on the supari, pocketing the empty pouch. 'The Machli Gala is...' With that, he launched into a long-winded explanation, at the end of which Suraiya could ace an exam on Pasinabad cuisine's biggest night out. 'Oh, it's a curtain raiser?'

DJ nodded. 'The Machli Gala is held a month *before* the Machli Stars are awarded to restaurants.'

'Ah! Noted, *Ustad* Saadat.' Suraiya gave an exaggerated bow.

DJ's eyes misted over. 'Your Ammi used to call me that when she was little.'

'You *were* a masterchef after all.'

DJ smiled sadly. 'I miss her so much.'

'She'll be back soon.' Suraiya reached out to pat his hand. 'I thought you'd be happy to have me over.'

'Zahenaseeb!' DJ took her hands into his and touched them to his eyes. 'Your first summer in Pasinabad. I'm so glad you convinced your Ammi.'

It was a *lot* of work, Suraiya had to admit. She'd always longed to visit her hometown. Secretly. And then, not so secretly. But Ammi wouldn't hear of it. 'Pasinabad's ancient history,' she'd say firmly. 'I'm so done with it.' She'd moved to the city a decade ago. And true to her word, never ever looked back. It was DJ who visited them every summer. DJ who'd tell stories about Pasinabad. Stories that would capture Suraiya's imagination and fill her heart with wonder. Not surprisingly, summer in Pasinabad became her birthday wish. Her New Year resolution. Her Mission Impossible. Which only became Mission I'mPossible when grandfather-granddaughter combined forces.

It had taken pretty-pleasing, pester power and prompt completion of homework and domestic chores (Suraiya), it'd taken persuasion (DJ), it'd taken tears, promises, bargaining (both Suraiya and DJ), before Ammi had given in.

'Not missing the city at all. So uncouth, uncultured, uncivilized.' Dada Jaan shuddered. 'Why couldn't your Ammi become a chef and take over the restaurant? But no, she had to become a naturist.'

Suraiya coughed politely. 'Um. Naturists are folks who roam around in their *birthday* suits.'

DJ's eyes widened in alarm.

'Ammi's a *naturalist*.'

'Khuda ka lakh-lakh shukr!'

As her grandpa offered heartfelt thanks heavenward, Suraiya went on, 'It's why she's away in the Amazon rainforest.'

'Hope Jungle Girl comes running home soon,' sniffed Dada Jaan. 'When she was your age, she'd run straight to the restaurant from school and demand Nimona Lajawaab with steaming hot jeera rice—'

'The what-mona?' Suraiya cut in, curiouser than a cat at a fish market.

DJ snapped out of the nostalgic trance he'd slipped into. A stricken look came over his face. It was brief-barely-there-blink-and-you'd-miss-it. But not for nothing was Suraiya known as Hawk Eye.

'Jeera rice,' DJ replied quickly.

'No, the other thing? This is the first I've heard of that dish. How come it's not on the menu? How come it's never made in the restaurant?'

'Coming!' DJ called out, swivelling towards the kitchen.

Ha! As if she'd fall for *that* ploy! She promptly fell into step with him. 'You were saying?'

'I was thanking my lucky stars your Ammi's not a naturist.'

'No, before that.'

'I was hoping she'd come home soon.'

'No, after that.'

'After what?' DJ batted his eyelashes innocently. 'I know I look young and handsome, but *hai*,' he flung a dramatic hand to his forehead, 'my memory's not what it used to be.'

Suraiya huffed. Dada Jaan's cooking days were behind him, but he could sure cook up an excuse. Something smelled fishy and it wasn't just the fish tikkas. He was trying to cover up something. But what? And why? First, the menu mystery. And now *this*. Suraiya cracked her knuckles. She was used to cracking stuff—knuckles, eggs, exams and once, quite by accident, Ammi's cell phone screen. Now it was time to crack the double mystery.

Out loud, she cooed, 'Must be tough, being a hundred years old.'

'Dhatt! Badmash!' DJ swatted at her in mock-outrage.

The grandfather clock in Suraiya's grandfather's restaurant (did that make it a *great grandfather* clock?) chimed in amusement. Suddenly, the kitchen doors flew open and Roshanara strode out with the tasting menu, an army of staff in tow.

'Didn't you say you had some great ideas to turn the place around?' Smartly, very smartly, DJ changed the subject.

A beaming Suraiya picked up her glittery notebook and reeled off all ten of them.

HOW TO LURE CUSTOMERS TO SHAAN-E-DAAWAT

1. Park elephant outside restaurant (Scratch that. Animal in captivity? Never!) Dress up as elephant and stand at entrance.
2. Start cab service to catch tourists right at their hotels.
3. Indian Welcome Ceremony. Band-baaja. Money garlands.
4. Free gift with every meal. Henna tattoos? Bindis? Clip-on nose ring?
5. Apply for Snake Charmer course. Under-13 category.
6. Apply for Bollywood Dance course? (Tricky. What if dancing skills are mandatory?)
7. Apply for Tourist Guide course. Ace Tourist Guide course by Tuesday.
8. Learn six foreign languages by next weekend.
9. Change menu (again).
10. Change look.

She looked around at the sea of stunned faces. 'So, what do you think?'

'Elephant? Cab service? Tourist guide?' asked DJ in a strangled voice.

'Tanik zyada hui gaya! Too much!'

'Seriously?' asked Roshanara.

'I want to change the look, at least,' Suraiya pushed on. Surely that was doable?

'What's wrong with your look?' asked DJ in bewilderment.

'Not my look! The restaurant's. Let's make it fresh and fun and Instagram-friendly. So, what do you say?'

After what seemed like an endless second, DJ nodded slowly.

'Yayyy!' She threw her arms around him.

5

Over-egging the Pudding

'AND THEN, I RAISED MY arms over my head,' Divumber looked around at the rapt audience, made up of charmed chefs, bewitched bawarchis, spellbound servers and devoted dish-washers, '...like a snake's hood!' He launched into Nagin Dance Version 2.0, taking turns to lunge at the faces of the mesmerized audience members, much to their giddy delight.

'Wah! Mere King Cobra!' someone crowed.

'*Hiss*-terical,' snorted Gajodhar.

Back in the day, Nawab Naak-Mein-Dum's kitchen boasted of expert Masalchis aka Spice Masters. Though Divumber couldn't tell cardamom from cinnamon, the restaurant was never short on masala and drama, because of this modern-day Spice Master. In fact, even if the entire world ran out of masala, Awadh Mahal would do just fine, thanks to him.

'You may have won this round. But to drum up more customers, we need solid ideas.' Gajodhar looked around. 'Thoughts?'

'Disco Nights?' suggested a junior bawarchi, who'd never been to a disco.

Gajodhar clicked his tongue. 'Where'd we even dance? On the gaddas?'

'Let's invite a famous singer every weekend,' proposed a music-mad server.

'How about a local DJ?' recommended the server, who was the DJ at every neighbourhood wedding.

'And who'd pay their hefty fees?' Gajodhar asked.

'A struggling poet, then?'

'Antakshari,' beamed an assistant chef, who couldn't sing to save her life. 'It's free.'

'Filmy music every weekend,' offered a dish-washer, who was a fan of all things Bollywood.

Divumber jotted down all the ideas on the chalkboard like a good leader.

1. **Disco Nights**
2. **Famous Singer**
3. **Local DJ**
4. **Struggling Poet**
5. **Antakshari**
6. **Bollywood music**

'How about karaoke?' suggested the Head Bawarchi.

Divumber added it to the list.

7. **Carry Okay**

'It's spelt K-A-R-A-O-K-E, okay?' snickered Gajodhar.

Divumber erased the wrong spelling with the back of his hand, cheeks red as Chukandar Chutney.

'What about you, Divumber?' asked Gajodhar.

'What about me?'

'Where's *your* idea?'

All eyes turned to Divumber.

'It's okay if you can't come up with an idea,' sniggered the Head Chef.

'How about something better? A great battle speech?' Snatching up a soaking wet lassi churner, Divumber brandished it like a sword. 'Brave soldiers, let's get ready to fight The Battle of Pasinabad. Awadh Mahal vs. The Rest. Real vs. Fake. Everyone's abandoned the Real Thing—the Pasinabad Pulao. Because it takes skill, time, patience. And so, they serve the ordinary, the *common* biryani to lure more customers.' He pretend-puked most violently into a freshly scrubbed kadhai.

Mataji had drilled it into Divumber from a very young age the many ways in which the iconic Pasinabad Pulao was superior to the generic biryani. While others his age learned multiplication tables, Divumber mugged up Mataji's Pulao vs. Biryani comparative study table.

'Who serves the Nawab's favourite, the original, the 100 per cent authentic Pasinabad Pulao?' Divumber roared, raising the lassi churner high, its wooden 'barrel' pointed to the sky. 'Awadh Mahal!' He chanted it like a war cry, stabbing the air with the churner.

'*And* Shaan-e-Daawat. Never underestimate the competiti—' Gajodhar broke off with a guilty grunt, as someone gate-crashed the gathering. 'Mataji!'

The staff greeted her politely.

'You're back!' Divumber greeted his dadi. He bowed low, before hopping off the stool to enthusiastic applause. 'Hey-ey-ey!' he bleated, as his granny herded him out like a stray goat, away from his durbar and adoring subjects.

Mataji led him to a little pavilion bang in the centre of the restaurant, which was modelled after Emperor Akbar's Anup Talao in Fatehpuri Sikri. This Talao's fountains, however, had long run dry. Its musicians had run away to the city in search of paying jobs. And all that was left was a payment counter with a high-backed maharaja throne, a modest cashier's chair, a heavy drop-safe for depositing cash and a framed poster listing The Rules. Mataji settled into her throne.

'What was all that drama in the kitchen? Got up to some sort of trouble again, didn't you? When your father was your age—uff!—he was a toofan, too!'

'What, me, trouble?' Divumber batted his long eyelashes. 'I was just motivating the troops with a battle speech. Like any good general would.'

Divumber was just under two weeks old in Pasinabad. Even so, he knew all about the Most Important (silent) Rule: *Thou Shall Not Mention the Enemy in Mataji's Presence*. What was that term Gajodhar kept using for Suraiya and her dada? Ah yes, 'persona non batata'! 'And please! I'm nothing like Papa. He's a climate *worrier*,' he added.

It's what Papa called himself. It's why he was always dashing around, trying to save the world. It wasn't going to save itself from destruction and pollution and humans, after all. But it bugged Divumber no end that Papa had always been too busy to take him to Pasinabad. It was fun to have Mataji over every summer, but still. Why did he have to wait all these years to visit his hometown? Was it so hard to tell the polar ice caps ta-ta-bye-bye for a week? Surely Papa could have taken a few days off? Sometimes, just sometimes, he felt Planet Earth was Papa's favourite child. Not him.

Divumber rolled his eyes, before continuing, 'Me? I'm a food *warrior*. HHHHHIIIIIIIYYYYYAAAAAHHHHHH!'

He let out a high-octane, high-decibel rallying cry as he high-kicked an imaginary opponent. Which would've been most spine-chilling, blood-curdling, toe-tingling if only it wasn't for—CHHHIIIIIRRRRRRR—the sound of the ripping fabric. There's a reason why martial artists wear saggy, over-sized pants. And Divumber had just discovered it.

'Hai-hai! Let me see,' Mataji tried to swivel him around to survey the damage. Divumber wiggled out of her grasp like a slippery eel, covering his posterior, his modesty and the wardrobe malfunction with both hands. 'I must depart. The border awaits my presence.'

'You must be the only general to fight a battle in torn pants,' Mataji said, cackling.

Divumber began walking backwards as if showing respect to a reigning begum. Never show your back to the monarch, as was the norm in the bygone era.

'You mean, *win* a battle in torn pants,' he declared, before beating a hasty retreat to the kitchen.

6

Something Smells Fishy

'WHAT ARE WE EVEN DOING here?' Roshanara groaned as she looked up at the signboard. *Mr & Ms Printing Company*, it announced brightly.

It was the next afternoon. They'd waited for DJ to leave for home, before speeding away in a fully loaded cycle rickshaw, all technicolour lights flashing and Bollywood chartbusters blaring. While the horse-drawn carriage had galloped away into the pages of history, a group of enterprising women—Tangewali Bhabhis—had kept the legacy of their ancestors alive, plying their vehicles for the locals, tourists, friends and neighbours (or should that be neigh-bours?)

'Told you, I want to see the menu. The one they claim *we* handed over,' said Suraiya, as they stepped into the dingy office. She didn't tell her cousin that she suspected 'Soggy Spinach' of sabotage. And that she was there to kick-start the investigation, on the prowl for proof.

Roshanara had called the office on the way, so the printers were ready with the menu. 'Here,' said Ms. Printer, handing it over.

Suraiya and Roshanara gasped. It was a sepia-coloured sheet! Not the eco-friendly handmade paper they'd painstakingly typed the menu on. And this one was folded like a hanky.

As Suraiya unfolded it, something slipped out of it and sailed to the floor. Something small, shiny, and silver. A strip of tinsel? A *clue*? Suraiya scooped it up gingerly and tucked it safely in her notebook. Then, she opened the menu with fumbling fingers. Sure enough, error after error, typo after typo greeted her.

'This isn't what we gave you!' she burst out.

'We've never seen this stationery before,' added Roshanara. 'Please try and remember. We gave you a transparent file with the menu tucked inside.'

'I remember,' said Ms Printer, defensively. 'But the next day, someone dropped *this* menu off in a big envelope. *Shaan-e-Daawat Menu. Final Version*, it said.'

Suraiya and Roshanara exchanged a shocked glance.

'Did you happen to see who it was?' Roshanara asked.

Ms Printer shook her head.

'Do you have the envelope, by any chance?' asked Suraiya hopefully, stuffing the mystery menu into her backpack.

'Why would I save an ordinary envelope?' scoffed Ms Printer.

'Do you remember what it looked like?'

'Why would I remember an ordinary envelope?'

Suraiya's face crumpled. They'd reached a dead end.

Just as they were turning around to leave, Ms Printer called out, 'Actually ... wait, it wasn't so ordinary.'

Suraiya whirled around. 'What?'

'The calligraphy. On the envelope.'

***

'What an afternoon,' Roshanara said, massaging her temples, when they were back in the tanga.

'Speaking of afternoon, funny story. DJ went into flashback mode and blurted something out...uh-what was it called?' Suraiya tapped her forehead, willing herself to remember the name of the mystery dish.

'What was *what* called?' asked Roshanara.

'That's what I'm trying to remember!'

As the tanga skidded to a halt at the bottle-necked Main Chowk, Suraiya spotted a familiar face at the traffic signal. Gullu Didi. In a burgundy Banarasi saree with a golden zari border, her hair pulled back in a bun, sporting a big bindi and a bigger smile. She clapped her hands and went from vehicle to vehicle, accepting small tokens of cash from the drivers and passengers, placing a blessing hand on their heads. 'Suraiya bitiya, Roshanara,' she said, waving.

The cousins called out a greeting. 'Where's Banno Didi? Haven't seen her in days,' asked Suraiya, looking around. Gullu Didi–Banno Didi were always together.

'Don't ask. She's down with pneumonia, the poor thing,' Gullu Didi said, her face clouding over.

But Suraiya's face lit up. Nimona! The cursed dish. 'Oh, yayyy!' she exulted.

Gullu Didi gaped at her. Roshanara squawked in shock.

'I mean, oh no! Hope Banno Didi feels better soon.'

Gullu Didi rotated both hands over Suraiya's head and touched them to her temples. She melted into the crowd as the traffic light turned green.

'Bewakoof! What was that "yayyy" all about?' chided Roshanara as they sped away.

'The name of the mystery dish.' Suraiya's eyes glittered. 'Nimona Lajawaab.'

To her amazement, Roshanara turned paler than Shahi Chicken Korma. 'Wh-what?'

'Ni-mo-na,' said Suraiya slowly.

'D-don't k-know what you're talking about.'

Suraiya had once walked in on Ammi downing Double ka Meetha like a video played on double speed. In the middle of the night. Right out of the long glass dish. A few hours after she'd enrolled in the swanky neighbourhood gym. Right when she was supposed to be on a fancy diet. Roshanara had the same expression now.

All around them, cars and buses belched smoke. And now, even Suraiya had steam coming out of her ears. First DJ, now Roshanara. Why was everyone acting so shady about the Nimona dish? What were they not telling her? Her hunch was right! There *was* another mystery afoot! Suraiya squared her shoulders. Well, there was more than one way to make people vomit the truth. 'That's not what I heard.' Suraiya shot Roshanara a meaningful look.

Her cousin's eyes widened.

'DJ couldn't bring himself to talk about it—'

'So, he said *I* could?' Roshanara shifted uncomfortably in her seat. 'How could he!'

That was easy, thought Suraiya with a satisfied smirk. She didn't even have to lie. Her cousin had put two and two together and come up with two-thousand-twenty-two.

'Tell me more about this Nimona thingy.'

'J-j-just stop saying that word already!'

'Oh, why? Sounds nice enough. Try it. Nimonanimonanimona—'

'Lalalalalalala!' Roshanara pressed her hands to her ears. 'Do what you want. You'll never get me to say Nimona. Ever!'

'Ha! You just did!'

'Uffo!'

'Come on, Rosh.'

'You really want to know, Su?'

'I reallyreally*really* do.'

'Fine, go ask Smelly Celery and his dadi.'

Suraiya's eyebrows flew to her hairline and remained there. What? Miserable Mushroom and his dadi knew about Nimona? The *enemy* was in on the secret? Her head whirled like a ceiling fan at full speed. What on earth was going on? The mystery kept getting knottier and knottier.

Roshanara wrung her hands and moaned. 'If-if I tell you, promise you'll stop saying it?'

Suraiya took her hand, a solemn look on her face.

Roshanara took a deep breath. 'Apparently, it used to be Dada Jaan's signature dish.'

'Ohhh!'

'But he stopped making it. Suddenly, abruptly, out of the blue.'

'Why?' cried Suraiya.

'Everyone thinks it's got something to do with Rotten Radish's family. But no one knows for sure. All we know is the recipe's cursed! Bad things happen when we speak of it! BAD things.'

7

Putting All Eggs in One Basket

SURAIYA'S MIND SPUN LIKE A lattu. What went down between DJ and Stinky Sugarcane's Dadi? How did the Nimona Lajawaab fit into the picture? Why did everyone think it was cursed? Had Awadh Mahal stolen the Nimona recipe? And a heartbroken DJ vowed never to make it again? Wait a stolen second! It was off Shaan-e-Daawat's menu, but what about Awadh Mahal's? Were they *still* making it? Serving it? How. Dare. They.

A loud wail broke into her thoughts. 'Tauba-tauba! What have I done!'

Suraiya felt a twinge of regret. Not because she was superstitious or anything. She knew that it was all mumbo jumbo. That there was no such thing as a cursed recipe. Weird recipes? Sure. Awful recipes? Most certainly. Jinxed recipes? Oh, come on!

But one look at her cousin and she knew she'd pushed things too far. Roshanara was distraught. 'Sorry, sorry,' she said sincerely, bumping shoulders with her. 'Didn't mean to upset you.'

As she consoled Roshanara, a store with flashy lights caught her eye. And a two-in-one idea flashed into her head. It'd solve:

1. **The Mystery of the Mis-spelt Menu**
2. **The Case of the Cursed Dish**

Suraiya leaned forward and called out over the booming *Badtameez dil, Badtameez dil, maane na mane na* (come to think of it, the song perfectly captured her mood), 'Bhabhi! Please stop at Chamko before you drop us home.'

'The Fancy Dress Store?' Roshanara yelped. 'Whatever for?'

A glint came into Suraiya's eyes.

'I know that look.' Roshanara juddered. 'Whatever's cooking in that mind of yours, the answer's no.'

'At least hear me out.'

'NO!' Roshanara burst out, after hearing Suraiya out.

'Please, Rosh. You're older, taller. You're perfect for the part.'

'NONONONONO! Can we please talk about something—*anything*—else? I don't want any trouble.'

'Don't worry, Rosh. Everything's going to be okay. There won't be any trouble.'

Suraiya had no idea—how could she, she wasn't a fortune teller or a crystal-ball gazer—that something *was* going to happen. Something big, something bad, something beyond bothersome. Trouble was on its way. And it was hurtling towards them at full speed.

***

Divumber and Gajodhar hurtled into the office of *Sign Us Pvt. Ltd.*

'You ruined our sign,' Divumber whined.

'We want a full refund,' Gajodhar demanded.

'Nothing doing,' snapped Mr Sign Us. 'It's all your fault.'

'Really?' cried Gajodhar. '*We* told you the name of our restaurant was AWFUL Mahal?'

'Yes! In that note you sent at the last minute.'

Divumber blinked. 'What note?'

'Forgot? You sent a small note. Inside a big envelope.'

'We didn't send anything!' exclaimed Divumber.

'Show me the envelope!' yelled Gajodhar.

Mr Sign Us patted his pockets. 'Right away, Your Majesties. I've been carrying it around, hoping you'd drop by.' He rolled his eyes.

Divumber plucked at Gajodhar's sleeve defeatedly. 'No use. Let's go.'

They were about to turn around when Mr Sign Us said, 'Wait. This fell out of the big envelope.' He dug into a drawer and tossed something at them.

Divumber caught it expertly. He squinted at the small, fluffy, pink ball. Was it a craft pom-pom? 'What *is* this?'

'How should I know?' snapped Mr Sign Us.

'The envelope he doesn't save. *That* he does,' muttered Gajodhar under his breath.

Sighing, Divumber dropped the pom-pom into his rucksack.

***

'What do you mean it's out of stock?' Suraiya whispered into the phone next morning. 'You were supposed to deliver it at home an hour ago,' she hissed, weaving her way through the crowded terrace, knocking into Khalas, pushing past Phuppos and colliding with Chachis drying their clothes.

Suraiya always thought of DJ's crumbling brick haveli as one big happy family hostel, packed as it was with an assortment of relatives.

'That was Chamko,' Suraiya murmured, disconnecting the call.

Roshanara wrung out her kameez. She gave it a good shake, looking like she wanted to give Suraiya a good shake. 'You promised, Su!'

'I didn't promise anything.'

'You tricked me! You let me believe you'd drop the plan if I told you the whole story.'

That was not the whole Nimona Lajawaab story, Suraiya wanted to retort. 'Anyway, Chamko can't send the lab coat, wig, security goggles across because—'

'The costume's out of stock,' a Khala cut in.

'Why did they promise home delivery then?' chimed in a Chachi. 'It's unacceptable.'

'Unreliable,' pouted a Phuppo. 'Unprofessional.'

The young chef dragged Suraiya away before more 'uns' could get aired on the airy terrace. 'You're playing with fire,' she said heatedly. 'If Dada Jaan gets wind of it...'

Suraiya shook her arm free. 'Cool down. The plan's off.'

'Good!' Roshanara stomped away towards the staircase.

Suraiya hmphed. As she glanced around the sunny terrace, her eyes fell on the washing line, on something blowing in the breeze. A crooked smile popped up on her face like a pimple.

***

Divumber casually glanced at the enemy territory and was pleasantly surprised. The entrance of Shaan-e-Daawat had been left unguarded. Ahaa! Maybe Suraiya had realized who was boss. Maybe she'd realized her restaurant was a lost cause. Maybe she'd had a bad bout of loosies after eating the stale fare they served at Shaan-e-Daawat. He was so busy chortling at his own joke, he nearly missed the customer who had stepped down from a cycle rickshaw and was tottering across the street.

The lady was walking in a rather ungainly fashion. And she seemed rather shor...Divumber stopped short. What was that word? Yes, *petite*. Papa was forever encouraging him to choose his words carefully, to be aware of their power, to replace them with gentler words, to build a kinder world for everyone. The petite lady was wearing a burkha with delicate zardozi embroidery and a mesh-screen niqab. A camera hung from one shoulder; a rucksack from the other.

As she lurched about like a newbie skier on a steep snowy slope, Divumber began flailing his arms like windmills to catch her eye. 'Ma'-aaaa-am! Ma'-aaaa-am!'

The lady began stumbling towards Shaan-e-Daawat.

'Sure you want to go in there, Ma'am? Guess what they give free with every meal?' Divumber clutched his tummy and pretend-puked his guts out. 'Want the real thing? Come on over!'

To make things easy for her, he grabbed her by the hand and began towing her inside Awadh Mahal.

He led her past the sea of white gaddas and bolsters laid out on the floor. Past the paintings of Nawab Naak-Mein-Dum gracing the wall. Past the traditional dastarkhwans on the faded carpets. Past the lavish spread on each bright tablecloth: huge platters piled high with mouth-watering varieties of Pulao; plates heaped with Butter Naans, juicy, tender Galouti Kebabs, smoky, succulent Mutton Keema; bowls overflowing with aromatic Chicken Korma and flavourful Salan; and earthen bowls with creamy Phirni topped with slivered almond and pistachio. Past guests seated cross-legged on the gaddas, tucking into the delectable spread.

'Have a seat, Ma'am,' said Divumber with a flourish as they reached an available gadda.

The lady shook her head, rooting around in her purse. She pulled out a phone and tapped on the screen. 'PISS! Which way to the kitchen?' came a prim and propah voice.

'*Excuse me*!' exclaimed Divumber. 'You want to do *what*? *Where*?'

8

Spill the Beans

THE WOMAN SHOOK HER HEAD vigorously.

'**P**asinabad **I**nstitute of **S**afety **S**tandards,' she clarified as she typed away on the screen again. 'PISS. I'm here for a health and safety risk assessment.'

Divumber perked up. 'Oh! You're a Food Safety Inspector?'

The woman nodded.

'This way, Ma'am.'

She jabbed the screen. 'Before that, may I see the menu?'

Divumber waved a dismissive hand as if asking for a menu at a restaurant was as ridiculous as asking for thermal underwear in the Sahara Desert. 'Almond Seera, Badam Halwa, Boondi Laddoo, Chicken Korma, Dahi Bada...' Divumber took off like Pasinabad Superfast Express, rattling off the dishes in alphabetical order.

The Food Inspector clicked her tongue. Waved her hands in his face. Snapped her fingers. Divumber, however, was on a roll. Somewhere between Lamb Kebab and Murgh Masallam, she finally managed to interrupt him with a loud, hacking cough. Taking a deep breath, she jabbed the screen again. 'Your Nimona Lajawaab. We've been getting complaints. Tons of them. About its quality and ingredients.'

A gamut of expressions flitted across his face. Confusion. Hesitation. Indecision. 'Namuna Lala Saab? Play that again, please?'

The woman went jab-jab.

'Wrong number, Ma'am!' he said, after listening to the voice again 'Must be some other restaurant. There's no such dish on our menu.'

The woman stabbed the screen impatiently. 'Nimona Lajawaab. Local delicacy.'

'Every delicacy on our menu is local. One second.' He darted away and came running back with the menu.

The woman's shoulders sagged as she scanned it.

'Now do you believe me?'

The woman placed her hands on her hips.

'I would've checked with my granny, but she's not here now. Wait, I'll get the Head Chef.' Divumber bounded towards the kitchen.

'Ma'am's here for PISS inspection,' Divumber explained, returning with Gajodhar.

The Head Bawarchi's eyes popped out in shock.

'Safety Inspector,' the voice explained.

'Oh!' Gajodhar welcomed the lady with a smile oilier than a jar of mango pickle.

She returned the greeting.

Before the Head Chef could make small talk, Divumber piped up impatiently, 'Nimona Lajawaab. Do we have it on the menu? No, na?'

Divumber expected the question to draw a blank stare. To his amazement, Gajodhar's eyes widened. Shock, alarm, distress flitted across his face. For only a nanosecond or two. Then, he blinked furiously. And his expression returned to the oilier-than-pickle setting. 'Never heard of it,' he brayed.

Divumber frowned. Thoughts popped up into his head like soap bubbles:

He does know something!

So, why's he playing dumb?

And what's with the constipated face? If that's acting, then the Taj Mahal is a branch of Awadh Mahal. Good thing the fellow doesn't want to be a movie star.

As the soap bubbles popped, Divumber turned to the PISS Inspector. 'Told you, Ma'am.'

'Our food's healthy and hygienic. Our kitchen, spic and span. Our ingredients fresh and ripe.' Gajodhar parroted like an advertisement.

'I'd like to inspect your kitchen, please,' the voice announced after a beat.

'After you. I mean, follow me.' Gajodhar led the way.

The Inspector made her way slowly, doddering on her laddery high heels.

'One minute, Ma'am.' The Head Bawarchi took a detour to the pavilion, 'Why don't I show you our Safe for Human Consumption certificate?' He slipped behind the counter and riffled through the top drawer of a cabinet.

Alas, The PISS Inspector took one step towards the pavilion and–HAWWWW!

The heel of her too-high sandals caught the hem of her too-long skirt. She swayed dangerously on her stilts, but before someone could reach out a steadying hand, she went crashing down! Her camera and rucksack followed, clattering and rolling across the floor.

Ever the gentleman, Divumber dive bombed for the spilled contents of her bag. Gajodhar bounded after the small, smiley squishy ball. A well-meaning guest retrieved a pen, a packet of wet wipes and a hairband. A well-placed server picked up a hand sanitizer that had landed in a most unsanitary spot.

'Are you okay?' an elderly guest asked, inspecting the fallen inspector.

The PISS Inspector nodded.

'Are you hurt?'

She shook her head, placing a hand on her heart.

Divumber gasped louder than her thumping heart. 'Wh-wh-what's this? "How to Lure Customers to Shaan-e-Daawat",' he read out loud from a glittery notebook.

Suraiya leapt up at the notebook, but thanks to the too-high heels and the too-long hem, she went down clutching air.

She'd been congratulating herself for coming prepared. For acting like royalty inside Awadh Mahal Royal Dining. Just so she could gain access to the menu, to the kitchen. In the hope of securing some proof, any proof that'd tie the Prickly Pumpkin to their wonky menu, to the cursed Nimona Lajawaab. But here she was, unmasked and exposed.

Divumber dropped the diary like a hot potato. Of all the sly, shifty, sneaky things! 'You're not a PISS Inspector. You're the criminal from next door!'

The royal dining restaurant looked royally shocked.

'Criminal? Where's the criminal?' bellowed a familiar voice.

All heads swung towards the towering, beefy policewoman as she leapt up from her gadda, like a wildflower in spring. 'Why worry when Inspector Chulbul's near, dear?'

'Arrest her!' Divumber beseeched, pointing an accusing finger at the PISS Inspector.

Suraiya struggled to her feet, leaning on the elderly guest for support. 'As if you're a statue of honesty!' she hissed, lifting the veil, dropping the act. 'What about our menu?'

There was pin-drop silence in the restaurant, other than the Suraiya–Divumber slanging match. Everyone was watching the proceedings like it was a war movie. The servers had stopped serving. The guests had stopped eating. One had started taking a video. Ignoring The Rules.

'What about it? What are you talking about?' Divumber said shrilly.

'You ruined our new menu. The royal cheek!' Suraiya raved.

For a moment, Divumber looked lost. 'Get lost! Don't you ever *ever* come back here again.'

'Or else?'

Divumber gulped. 'W-w-wait and watch.'

Suraiya bunched her fingers into a fist, taking a menacing step forward. 'Tell me now.'

'I give the orders around here, okay.' Divumber stepped back. Just in case.

The scene would be discussed, dissected, embellished, exaggerated for generations to come. By an assortment of assistants, a bevy of bawarchis, a slew of servers, a gaggle of guests, a posse of police-people.

In one account, Suraiya would holler, 'I know you're nothing like us, but this is too much!'

And Divumber would screech, 'I agree! We're way better than you.'

In another, they'd launch themselves on the other, tearing each other apart like angry beasts.

In yet another, Inspector Chulbul would struggle to separate them.

In all the versions, storytellers and listeners would unanimously agree that Pasinabad had turned into a combat zone. That the Great Pulao War had undeniably broken out.

9

Crying Over Spilt Milk

'THAT FOUL FENUGREEK!' SURAIYA SNIFFED as she chopped onions. A whole day had passed since the showdown, but she was still in a foul mood. Caught red-handed, she'd returned home empty-handed. No proof. Nothing. As for the 'clue' she'd picked up at the Printer's, Suraiya had no clue what it was. She'd stared at the small, shiny, silvery, not-tinsel long into the night. Examined it from all angles. But it was no go. Where had it come from? What was it doing in the menu? Was it even a clue? Or was she reading too much into it?

'I never should've gone to Awadh Mahal.'

Roshanara tossed her head, grinding cinnamon and cardamom to a fine powder. Suraiya heard the silent 'I told you so' loud and clear.

'Do you know how hard it was? Keeping mum? Holding on to my temper? I've never been so mad undercover.' Suraiya sniffed, feeling very sorry for herself. And yet, she hadn't blown her lid off. With a self-control she didn't know she possessed, she'd willed herself to calm down. She'd taken huge risks to pull off the stunt, after all:

- Pinching a Khala's outfit (or was that a Phuppo's?)
- Borrowing Roshanara's high heels (worst decision ever)
- Dipping into the Emergency Funds Ammi had given her (travelling solo had meant footing the bill for a Tangewali Bhabhi cycle rickshaw)

Because it was her only opportunity to sneak into the enemy camp. Business was lean on Tuesdays as Pasinabad Bazaar was closed on Tuesdays. But since stomachs don't take weekly offs, here they were, working. As for DJ, he'd taken the morning off to dye his hair, moustache and beard for an upcoming family wedding. It was a tedious, tiresome, time-consuming event. The dyeing process, that is, not the family wedding. But as DJ always said, 'You can't turn back the clock, but that shouldn't stop you from trying.'

Suraiya passed the chopped onions to Roshanara. 'Even when that Dreadful Drumstick *hand*cuffed me and dragged me inside like a broken airport trolley, I kept calm and snooped on.' *Maybe that wasn't such a bad thing,* said the little voice in her head. *Those heels weren't meant for walking down potholed streets. Scratch that – they weren't meant for walking.*

Roshanara added the cinnamon-cardamom powder, ghee and salt to the minced meat and kneaded it thoroughly. 'Why did you go next door at all?'

Suraiya wasn't ready to share her suspicions about the menu sabotage. So, she said the next best thing. 'I was trying to find out more about the Nimona Lajawaab.'

A hush fell over the bustling kitchen. All activity ground to a halt. A server sent a silent prayer heavenwards. Another crossed himself. Stress crackled like a stove fire.

'But the Lousy Leek looked blank. He'd never heard of the dish. Didn't look like he was hiding something.' Suraiya huffed, passing Roshanara a bowl of ginger-garlic paste.

She'd gone to Awadh Mahal looking for proof, only to find a surprise waiting for her. Her mouth had dropped open the minute she set foot inside. Awadh Mahal was nothing like Shaan-e-Daawat. Her family restaurant was, well, family friendly. It played host to all kinds of families. Big families, small families, noisy families, squabbling families.

At Awadh Mahal, however, all she could spot were couples, solo diners, tourists and even a firangi tourist. There were no long wooden tables that were just right for a family celebration. No high chairs to feed a fussy child. Only gaddas, carpets and dastarkhwans. The restaurant looked different. Not in a bad way, though.

Clearly, she'd underestimated the competition, she admitted to herself in a rare moment of humility. If *she* of all people was tempted to flop down on the inviting-looking gadda and stuff her face, imagine how a real customer would feel there!

Lost in thought, Suraiya picked up a nasty-smelling bark from a bowl.

'Careful,' Roshanara shrieked. 'That's Behosh, a rare spice. Sniffing it raw can knock you out cold.' She turned to a junior chef. 'Go keep it in the pantry. Told you to be careful!'

Suraiya promptly dropped the spice back in the bowl. 'Sorry, everyone, I shouldn't have mentioned the cursed dish,' she said sincerely, hoping to dissolve the tension in the kitchen.

Roshanara nodded, seasoning rice with salt and cardamom-cinnamon powder, before going on to parboil it. 'But how did you change your voice?'

Suraiya smiled weakly. 'BOLO – the Text to Speech app.'

'When did you even download it?' Roshanara walked over to another junior chef, who was frying the meatballs in ghee.

'After you went to sleep.' Suraiya had stayed up, downloading the BOLO app on the emergency phone Ammi had given her, checking out the features, trying out different voices, doing a dry run.

'That was some trick you played on the neighbours.' Roshanara placed a big handi on low flame, added a layer of rice, followed by a layer of meatballs, followed by a splash of rose water and saffron milk. 'And what about Phoolkanta Devi? Where was she when all this drama was going on?' Roshanara went on to repeat the process. Another layer of rice, meatballs, rose water, saffron milk.

Suraiya blinked. 'Oh, you mean Greasy Ginger's Dadi? She was away.'

'Oh! And then?'

'And then, it was qayamat.'

It *had* felt like the end of the world. She'd fallen on the floor. Her notebook had fallen into enemy hands. And the sky had fallen in.

10

The Big Cheese

'SO, THIS NAMUNA LAATSAAB,' DIVUMBER began, trying to drum up a new trick to get Gajodhar to talk. About the mystery dish. Why did the PISS *Imposter* Suraiya go to great lengths to learn about it?

'Nimona Lajawaab,' said Gajodhar without thinking.

A triumphant look came over Divumber's face. To his surprise, Gajodhar leapt to his feet and began doing sit-ups, holding his ears criss-cross, muttering, 'Sorry, sorry, sorry,' he looked skywards. 'Look what you've done! You made me utter a bad word!'

'Ninoma Lapata?' asked Divumber innocently. 'A bad word?'

'Nimo...ufff!' Gajodhar caught himself in the nick of time. 'Cursed word. Cursed dish. Cursed recipe.'

'Cursed?' Divumber said incredulously. 'How? By whom? Why?'

'I know I'm the smartest person in here, but even I don't know everything.'

Before Divumber could pester him further, a commotion erupted outside. He ran to the entrance. Out of the corner of his eyes, he spotted Suraiya outside Shaan-e-Daawat.

A fancy, glossy, tank of a car pulled into the narrow street, like a hippo squeezing into a tutu. Cyclists honked in displeasure, pedestrians ducked into shops, cows mooed in disapproval. As the car braked to a halt, two men in black safari suits and dark glasses hopped out of the cavernous car. Man in Black One held the door open. Man in Black Two reached in and heaved an elderly man out of the low seat like a metal trunk. The metal trunk was wearing a dhoti kurta, dark glasses and more jewellery than a jewellery shop window (layered chain, thick bracelet, single dangly earring and gemstone rings). He twirled his grey handlebar moustache and strode briskly towards the restaurants.

Divumber and Suraiya both dashed forward to 'usher' him inside. Divumber beat her to it in a photo-finish. Wrapping his hand around the elderly man's wrist like a handcuff, Divumber began to drag him inside. For a nanosecond, the scene froze. Then everything happened in fast forward. The Men in Black immediately pointed their finger guns at him, barking, 'Hands above your head, drop to your knees, get on the ground!' Before Divumber could obey, they'd rugby-tackled him to the ground!

A shell-shocked Divumber let out a screech. The traffic came to a screeching halt. A passing cow dropped a heap of dung on the street.

The doors of Awadh Mahal flew open. Mataji hobbled out. 'Nooooo!' she cried. 'That's my grandson. From the city. First visit in eleven years. He didn't know, my sincere apologies.'

The doors of Shaan-e-Daawat flew open. Suraiya's Dada Jaan shuffled out. 'Nahiii!' he cried theatrically, needlessly. 'That's my grand-daughter—'

'From the city. Visiting Pasinabad for the first time ever,' cut in Suraiya, cool as an ice cube.

'I humbly apologize on her behalf,' said Dada Jaan.

Suraiya scowled. 'Tell me again why we're apologizing to Mr Whoever-He-Is.'

'You don't know Badke Bhaiya?!' The Men in Black glared at her (at least, it felt like they were glaring at her. She couldn't be sure because of the dark glasses). 'The most legendary figure in Pasinabad!'

Suraiya gasped. Divumber gasped louder. They'd arrived only about a fortnight ago, but even *they* had heard of Badke Bhaiya. Who hadn't? He was the biggest don of Pasinabad, after all. He'd made millions overnight, the only way millions could be made overnight (except by winning the lottery. And no, he hadn't won the lottery): by breaking the law, by breaking the hearts of innocent, trusting, unsuspecting folk, by breaking the bones of anyone who dared to get in the way.

Behind his back, people called him 'briber', 'cheater', 'two-faced', 'don', 'double crosser'. To his face, they called him Real Estate Raja, Business Baron, Tireless Tycoon, Model Millionaire.

'I-I thought someone was trying to "off" me,' squeaked the most powerful man in Pasinabad, shaking like a newborn's rattle. An attack on one's life can have that effect on a person, don or no don. 'Let the boy go,' panted the crook, straightening up slowly.

The Men in Black dropped Divumber to the ground like a gunny bag.

A groaning Divumber was pulling himself up when Badke Bhaiya rasped, 'Joint meeting. With Shaan-e-Daawat and Awadh Mahal. NOW!'

***

Minutes later, they were all seated. On gaddas. Around a dastarkhwan. Spread on a long table. In the middle of the street. The gaddas and tablecloth came from Shaan-e-Daawat. The table, from Awadh Mahal. The narrow street was courtesy of Pasinabad.

The genteel folk of Pasinabad were used to blocked streets, to being stranded on the road for hours. Especially during election season, when netas gave rousing speeches from makeshift stages constructed thoughtfully in the middle of the street. This was the first time a street was closed to traffic because of a non-neta. But the townsfolk had no choice except to grumble, grouch, gripe and put up with it.

'No formalities, please. Don't go to any trouble.' Badke Bhaiya flashed an oily smile.

Suraiya snorted rudely. Divumber smiled politely. Everyone knew the don's protests were as insincere as a neta's promises. Naturally, Mataji and Dada Jaan dutifully dismissed them and motioned to their staff. Item after delectable item, delicacy after scrumptious delicacy appeared on the dining spread. The iconic Pasinabad Pulao. Kebabs. Kalia. Korma. Shorba. Salan. Tall glasses of tantalizingly refreshing Jal Jeera topped with ice cubes.

After the feast was laid out, Badke Bhaiya heaped a large platter and offered it to Divumber and Suraiya.

'Sorry, would've loved to. But I'm too stuffed. Big breakfast,' Divumber explained apologetically. He burped loudly to prove his point.

'No, thanks,' said Suraiya curtly.

'It wasn't a request,' the crook snapped.

Divumber's eyes flew to Mataji, who nodded gently.

Suraiya's eyebrows flew up. Dada Jaan shot her an encouraging look.

The feuding foodies gulped. Then, they proceeded to gulp down a bit of, well, everything.

'In my line of work, one can't be too careful,' declared the don, as the bitter rivals handed the platter back to the guest.

An empty platter and a full tummy later, the don got down to business.

'What brings you here?' asked Mataji, offering him a sweet paan.

'The future.'

'A time machine?' Divumber grinned, and then sobered up when no one laughed.

'As you know, I'm a dreamer.'

'Among other things,' muttered Suraiya under her breath.

'My new dream? To build the first ever food court in Pasinabad! Serving all kinds of—'

'Junk food?' Suraiya pulled a face.

'Fast food. The word is fast food.'

'That's two words,' Suraiya sneered.

'Just imagine,' Badke Bhaiya went on, a faraway look in his eyes. 'One destination. For every kind of temptation. Pizzas, burgers, pastas, noodles, cakes, pastries, breads...'

'...cavities,' said Suraiya in a loud whisper.

'I've even zeroed in on the location.' The crook looked at them meaningfully.

Everyone blinked. A gasp went up as realization dawned.

'You mean...?' began Mataji.

'Where our restaurants stand?' finished Dada Jaan.

'Brilliant, isn't it?' Badke Bhaiya exulted. 'So, what do you think, Phoolo and Saad?'

Divumber and Suraiya stood rooted in horror. How casually he'd addressed Dada Jaan and Mataji! As if this was a social visit. When, in fact, the crook was trying to seize their restaurants by hook or crook!

11

In a Pickle

SURAIYA GLANCED AT DADA JAAN. He looked as if he'd gone from one hundred years to two hundred in two seconds.

Divumber sneaked a peek at Mataji. She looked pale, like a bowl of perfectly set curd.

'Arrey, I thought you'd jump at the offer. It can't be easy running the restaurants at your age.'

Mataji bristled. Dada Jaan prickled. Was the crook calling them old? To their face? Even Suraiya and Divumber looked mildly offended.

'Look at it this way. It'll save you the trouble of paying the rent. Which, as you know, you're behind on. You could always look for a cheaper place to move to.'

Mataji took off her glasses and blew on them, before wiping them on her saree pallu. 'Awadh Mahal isn't a restaurant.'

Divumber's brow knitted. 'It isn't?'

'It's a forty-year-old legacy.' Mataji's voice was soft but firm.

'Shaan-e-Daawat is not a restaurant,' said Dada Jaan, his voice thick. 'It's a Pasinabad landmark.'

'It'd be such a shame if we shut down,' said Mataji. 'Think about our patrons.'

'They'd be heartbroken if it shutters down,' added DJ.

Badke Bhaiya cast a withering glance in the direction of the empty restaurants. 'Right. Your die-hard *patrons*.' Sarcasm dropped from his voice, like oil from a poori.

'It's Tuesday!' Suraiya said hotly.

'Tuesday or Sunday, these days people like to eat modern food,' retorted the crook. 'Who eats boring oily biryani anymore?'

'Not boring oily biryani,' Divumber pointed out politely, 'boring oily *Pasinabad Pulao*.'

'Same difference.'

Mataji and Dada Jaan stiffened. Had he really just compared the generic biryani to the iconic Pasinabad Pulao! Biryani was just biryani. Pasinabad Pulao was ... an experience!

'Learn from your neighbours. They did the right thing.' Badke Bhaiya jerked his head at the abandoned building next door. Suraiya and Divumber knew he was talking about Fillum Talkies. The single-screen cinema theatre next door used to be a Pasinabad hotspot, but now shiny new multiplexes had stolen their limelight and customers. And sadly, instead of 'Lights, Camera, Action', it was 'lights out' at the legendary landmark. A summer loo (not washroom, scorcher of a breeze) had started to blow, but Suraiya shivered. Divumber shuddered. Were their grandparents' restaurants doomed to meet the same fate?

Badke Bhaiya held out his hands. The Men in Black rushed over to heave him up.

'Don't rush into making a decision,' the don said generously. 'Take your time. Think it over.'

'We *have* thought it over and our answer is no,' declared Suraiya, springing to her feet. Dada Jaan tugged at her sleeve gently.

'We'll pay this month's rent on time, pinky promise,' pleaded Divumber, leaping to his feet.

The swindler gave him a stinky look. 'And what about the rent of the last six months?'

'That, too,' said Suraiya. 'We'll get our customers back somehow.'

Divumber bobbed his head.

Badke Bhaiya stared at Suraiya and Divumber with sharkish eyes. 'Okay done! I'll give you a month. If you don't clear your dues by then, you'll clear out.'

'And if we don't?' Suraiya asked, a hint of challenge in her voice.

An uncomfortable silence fell.

'Oh, I have my ways to get people to do what I want.'

'And if we do clear our dues? Then we can stay on, right?' asked Divumber.

'Then I'll never ask you to vacate again.' Badke Bhaiya threw his head back and laughed a hearty laugh. Careful not to offend him, everyone joined in rather nervously, until he began choking on his saliva. It took the Men in Black a few well-timed thumps to get him to stop.

***

'Don't panic,' Suraiya told Roshanara (and herself) that night.

A soft snore told her Roshanara was fast asleep. Sighing, she reached for the emergency phone.

'Ammi?'

'Su?' her mother answered groggily. 'Is everything okay?'

Oops! Suraiya bit her tongue. She'd forgotten about the time difference.

'Y-y-yes! Sorry sorry! W-w-will talk in the morning...'

'All good, sweet pea? You sound worried.'

Continents away and still, Ammi knew!

'Okay, guess what? I have a surprise for you.'

Suraiya pressed the phone to her ear. She could really use a good surprise.

'What do you say to moving to California? Got a great job offer from a prestigious university last week. Have been talking to some friends and...'

'You're getting married, aren't you?' Suraiya shrilled.

'*What?!* Whatever made you think that?'

It had happened to one of Suraiya's classmates. And ever since, she'd been on high alert.

'You're hiding stuff from me! I just know it!'

'Su, I never ever wanted to get married,' Ammi said firmly.

'Never ever?'

Ammi hesitated.

'See, you're hiding stuff.'

'Fine. I did come close to it once,' Ammi said softly.

Suraiya's eyes widened. 'But?'

There was a spot of silence. 'Your Dada Jaan didn't approve...it was complicated...and-and a long time ago,'

Ammi said gruffly. 'Anyway, I have you. I don't need anyone else. Promise you'll think about the move?'

Suraiya exhaled. 'Okay, Ammi.'

***

'Don't worry,' Suraiya told Dada Jaan (and herself), the next morning. 'We'll find a way.'

DJ was moping around the restaurant. 'I'm out of options, meri jaan,' he said, chewing resignedly on his supari. 'Looks like I'll have to sell the haveli to pay off the dues.'

Suraiya stared at him in horror. Was he seriously considering selling the roof over his head? Where would he go? Where would the Phuphos-Khalas-Chacha-Chachis go?

'What shall I do next month? And the month after that?' DJ patted Suraiya's hand as if to console her (and himself). 'Perhaps Badke Bhaiya has a point. Perhaps I should cut my losses and wind up. So many hidden costs, overheads. Running a restaurant is *not* easy. It's like making a hippo exercise. Perhaps it wouldn't be such a bad idea to wind up, after all. I could always do something else.'

Suraiya swallowed the lump in her throat. What would DJ do? Cooking was his only passion. Sadly, frequent bouts of illness had left him too weak and frail to stand in the kitchen for long hours. What if he lost the restaurant, too?

DJ rubbed his forehead. 'I could take up a job. But who'd hire me at the ripe old age of—' he stopped mid-sentence.

Careful not to upset him further, she said, 'You don't look a day over...uh...ninety?'

'I could always learn a new hobby. Knitting, maybe?'

Suraiya coughed. DJ was many things: kind, generous, creative, moody, always stylish, occasionally forgetful, and, like most brilliant chefs, bad-tempered. But patient he was not.

'I don't see a way out.' DJ chewed his supari slowly.

Your Ammi's not interested in running Shaan-e-Daawat. She's made that abundantly clear.'

It'd be difficult to run the restaurant from thousands of kilometres away, mused Suraiya. (She'd decided to let Ammi tell DJ about the Big Move to California.)

'Unless *you*'re keen on running it when you're older...?' Dada Jaan left the question hanging.

'Hate to disappoint, but I want to become a hacker when I grow up. The good kind.'

'Ah, yes. You mentioned,' DJ said ruefully. 'The ones who do the wrong thing for the right reason.'

Suraiya nodded. 'Right.'

'What am *I* going to do? With you and Ghazal far away—'

'You could always move with us?'

DJ smiled sadly. 'I'm too old to live anywhere but home.' He looked around the restaurant. 'And this, this is home away from home.'

It was true. DJ practically lived in the restaurant (except when he went home to nap).

'Let's not give up hope.' She took DJ's hand in hers. 'Something *will* work out. I'm sure of it.'

12

Eating Humble Pie

DIVUMBER COULDN'T STOP THINKING ABOUT the looming threat. He knew they'd stalled Badke Bhaiya for the moment. But time was running out. And so was money. Mataji had confessed that she was struggling to keep the restaurant afloat. 'Bank loan!' he shouted excitedly. Papa had taken one out last year to buy the flat they were currently living in.

Mataji let out a defeated sigh. 'Too many debts. The kothi's mortgaged. No one's going to give me a loan.'

Kothi. The word made Dadi's house sound all grand and stately. In truth, the one-storey building was only slightly more rundown than their restaurant. Divumber knew Papa could help. But he also knew his granny was too proud to ask Papa. It was down to him to solve the problem. But how?

Shoulders slumped, Divumber dragged himself to the backdoor. As he pushed it open, he spotted a copy of *Petu Times* wedged between the dumpster and the wall. He plucked it out with nimble fingers and gasped. ***Awadh Mahal Should Be Renamed Washout Mahal!*** jeered the headline.

Another stinker of a review! This one, by someone called The Hangry Glutton.

Right then, the backdoor of Shaan-e-Daawat swung open and Suraiya walked out, carrying a large platter of leftovers. As she put the food out on the low gully wall, Divumber simmered, seethed, steamed up. Finally, boiling over, he did the unimaginable, the unthinkable, the *un*possible: he marched over, covering the distance between the two restaurants in a few long lunges.

'Hope you're happy now!' he hissed.

Suraiya's head shot up. She spun around to face him so fast she nearly lost her balance. 'What's wrong with you?!' she shrieked, as the platter crashed to the floor.

'What's wrong with *you*?' Divumber held up the newspaper in front of her accusingly.

'What's this?' Her eyes widened as she read the headline. Her eyes skimmed over the restaurant review. 'Wait,' she said slowly when she finished reading, 'you think *I* have something to do with it?'

He glowered at her. 'I *know* you have something to do with it.'

She sucked in a breath as her eyes fell on another headline. Right below the Awadh Mahal's review.

'Shun-E-Daawat!' she read out loud. "Having a meal at Shaan-e-Daawat felt like being lost in a deep, dark jungle. Temper tantrums, tears of exhaustion, thrashing and screaming at the top of the lungs—and that was just the grown-ups. Herds of children running free and wild, faces and clothes covered in gravy, like cheetahs across the grasslands. Snarling parents chasing after them. Shrieking servers spilling food (spilled because of accidents) and tears (spilled not-so-accidentally). I'd have thought about leaving the moment I entered. Sadly, I couldn't hear my own thoughts over the sound of all the bawling-brawling-growling-howling. Nor could I take a step without stepping on a diaper. Or puke. The entire experience was as close to enjoyable as jail is to fun." Suraiya's head reeled as she came to the end of the review.

Divumber's jaw dropped (and so did the newspaper). 'Your restaurant got a horrible review, too? Who *is* this mean reviewer?'

'For all I know, it's you,' Suraiya said through gritted teeth.

'You really think I'd give *my* restaurant a nasty review?!'

Fair point, mused Suraiya.

Without warning, the back doors of Shaan-e-Daawat creaked open. Suraiya quickly shoved Divumber behind a dumpster and gave a fake cheery smile to the server carrying two bulging black bags. She waited until he disposed of the trash and went back inside the restaurant.

Whew! That was close. She couldn't be seen talking to the enemy. If someone found out... If DJ found out... Suraiya couldn't bring herself to finish the thought. She thumped on the dumpster.

'We can't talk here,' she snapped, as Divumber came out of his hiding place. Spinning around, she scooted through the narrow gully to the neighbouring building. Divumber bounded after her.

'Fillum Talkies?' Divumber squeaked as Suraiya slipped her hand inside through the broken window and unlatched the back door.

'Coming or not?' Her voice echoed as she walked inside.

Divumber hesitated. Was he really going to do this? Break into an abandoned cinema hall? To chat with the enemy? But then, the Mystery of the Rotten Reviews called (or was that Suraiya again?) and he ducked inside.

'Who'd do such a thing?' Suraiya wondered out loud, when they were seated on the stage.

'The Freeloader Mafia?'

Suraiya goggled. 'Who?'

'Food influencers we turned away. They could've done it out of spite.'

'Or, it could be a real, actual customer. Someone who really, actually hated our restaurants.'

'So much that they dashed off a rotten review to a newspaper?' asked Divumber. People had too much free time. Why couldn't they just burp and move on? 'You know what I'd do after visiting an awful restaurant? Never visit it again. Ever.'

'Me too,' said Suraiya.

It was tough to say who was surprised more by the confession. Was it possible? Could sworn enemies agree on something?

'You know, this isn't the first time someone's attacked Awadh Mahal.'

'Same,' said Suraiya. 'Someone's out to get Shaan-E-Daawat, too.' She recounted the menu mayhem.

'Ganji ke Vade? Nargisi Kurta? Kutta Curry?' Divumber clucked as she rattled off the items on the wonky menu.

How sad for Suraiya and her Dada. The thought sprang up into his head uninvited, unexpected. Why should he care?

Why should he feel bad for his enemies? And yet, there it was, that slight twinge of sadness.

'Wait till you hear what happened to us.' He narrated the signboard saga.

'How unfortunate,' Suraiya said when he finished. To her surprise, she meant it.

'I did wonder if you were behind the attacks,' Divumber admitted.

'And I was *sure* you were the culprit,' Suraiya confessed.

They broke off with awkward, hesitant half-smiles (or should that be a full smile? Because two halves make a whole?).

Suraiya yelped as a startling thought struck her. 'Wait! What if the attacks are related?'

Divumber's mouth formed an O. 'As in, the same person's out to get us *both*?'

13

The Moon Is Made of Green Cheese

SURAIYA NODDED GINGERLY.

Divumber scratched his chin. 'What if these "attacks" aren't attacks at all? What if it's just a—'

She held up a hand. 'Don't say it's a coinci—'

'Coincidence.'

'Three times in a row?' Suraiya scoffed. 'Even a toddler would have a hard time believing that.'

Divumber scratched his head. 'But who'd gun for us?'

Gun! The wheels in Suraiya's head began turning extra fast. And a name popped up like mustard seeds in oil. 'Badke Bhaiya?'

Divumber's eyes widened. 'Why would he do something like this? We promised to vacate if we can't make the rent this month.'

'To force us to shut shop sooner? To make sure that we leave? Didn't he say he had his own ways to get people to obey him?' Maybe he's worried? That we'll get tons of customers and turn things around?'

The theatre fell utterly silent and still. Except for the squeak-squeak-scurry-scurry of rats.

'I wish I'd brought my notebook along.'

'We can make notes here,' Divumber tapped his head.

And that's exactly what they did.

MYSTERY OF THE MENU MAYHEM / SECRET OF THE SIGNBOARD SAGA / RIDDLE OF THE ROTTEN REVIEWS

SUSPECT: Badke Bhaiya

MOTIVE: To arm-twist us into shutting shop

CLUE: His own words

'Gajodhar thinks all this is happening because of a cursed recipe.'

Suraiya pulled a face. 'Not the Nimona Lajawaab I came to snoop about?'

'One and the same,' Divumber confirmed. 'Everyone goes nuts if I so much as mention it.'

'Same story at our restaurant.' Suraiya rolled her eyes. 'So silly,' she said in the voice Ammi usually reserved for lecturing her. She hesitated, before asking, 'Want to find out who's behind these attacks together?'

Divumber raised an eyebrow. 'You mean, team up?'

'Look, I don't like this anymore than you do,' she said candidly. 'But there's no time to lose. We have only a month to catch the culprit.'

'And pay off all the dues.'

She nodded grimly. 'Let's meet here? In the afternoons? But what are we going to tell them?' She motioned in the direction of the restaurants.

Divumber mulled it over. 'I'll tell everyone I've signed up for a summer course.'

'Me too.' Suraiya rubbed her hands in anticipation. 'Now all I need to do is win the Machli Star and—' she broke off mid-word, eyes widening in dismay.

Divumber's eyes lit up. 'A Machli Star would be awesome!' Gajodhar had told him all about it. He could see it in his mind's eye. Customers queuing up all the way to Kolkata, Kulu-Manali, Kanyakumari. 'We'll come up with a dish so marvellous, so glorious, so wonderous, the tastebuds of the Machli Star experts won't stand a chance.'

A thunderous look came over Suraiya's face. 'The Machli Star's going to be Shaan-e-Daawat's. Ours and ours alone. It's my idea!' So blunderous. She'd let the big idea slip. Now he was going to try to bag one, too. That's all she needed. More competition. From *the* competition.

'Ideas are like the wind. You don't own them,' said Divumber grandly. 'If you're going to be like this—'

Suraiya was already on her feet. 'You know what? I don't need your help to save my restaurant.'

'Me neither.'

They stomped away to the backdoors of their restaurants without a backward glance.

***

'Silly, foolish, *dumb* idea,' Suraiya chided herself as she scribbled furiously in her notebook later that week. What was she thinking? Partnering with that Pesky Pumpkin, of all people! And worse, she'd given away her secret weapon.

The Machli Star. Of course, there was the small matter of winning the Star, but Suraiya was confident that with a little bit of out-of-the-box thinking and a lot of hard work, Shaan-e-Daawat would bag the top honour.

'Who's dumb?' asked Roshanara, as her cycle rickshaw pulled up outside the restaurant the following morning.

'No one,' Suraiya said quickly. 'I-um, I meant Dum. You know, the slow style of cooking? The one we use for Pasinabad Pulao and all our dishes.'

'Hmm.' Roshanara turned to Tangewali Bhabhi, handing a bunch of crisp notes to her.

Suraiya made a beeline for the restaurant, only to stop cold. 'Eeek! Is that blood?' She stared in shock at the red stains on the entrance wall. Where did they come from? Before she could wonder and ponder, a server came bounding out of Shaan-e-Daawat.

'It's gone! Our history's gone.'

Suraiya dashed into the restaurant and looked around wildly. There was stunned silence, a sea of shocked faces, one speechless DJ, but *no* bronze plaque!

Suraiya opened her mouth to let out a blood-curdling, ear-splitting, toe-curling scream.

***

Divumber matched her decibel for decibel. At the same time.

That morning, there were a few things on his to-do list:

1. Get better ideas to save restaurant from Badke Bhaiya
2. Get more customers

3. Get Papa to visit Pasinabad (and get fresh pairs of underwear along)
4. Get to the bottom of the menu-signboard mystery

But now, another shocking entry had been added to it:

5. Get the missing bronze plaque back!

14

The Fat Is in the Fire

'A THEFT MOST FOUL!' SHAAN-E-DAAWAT and Awadh Mahal bemoaned.

'Did someone say theft?' piped up a loud voice. And Inspector Chulbul swept up their doorstep like an unannounced flash flood. 'The name is Bul. Chul-bul.'

The next thing Suraiya and Divumber knew, they were out on the street attending another blocked-road meeting. This one organized by those on the *right* side of the law.

The air was heavy with the promise of fennel-coriander-onions-ginger-garlic cooking in mutton stock. But all everyone could smell was fear.

Inspector Chulbul paced about, her sunglasses fixed on the back of her collar. A hawaldar bumbled over with a paan. She popped it into her mouth. 'Let me shee if I've got thish right,' she said, tapping her danda on her palm.

Everyone blinked. Leaned forward. Strained their ears.

'Pardon?' asked DJ.

'You are pardonedsh.' The cop spat the betel juice out by the side of the road. Then, she swung around dramatically to point the danda at DJ and Mataji. 'You! And you! Your nameplates are gone?'

'Plaque, plaque,' Suraiya corrected her, bristling. She did not just call the historical honour a *nameplate*!

The Inspector tch-tched. 'Don't you brush your teeth twice daily? Morning and night?'

'No! I mean, yes! Yes, I brush—'

Divumber rushed to explain. 'As in, our *historical artefacts* have gone missing.'

The cop gave a brisk nod. 'I was coming to that.' She stalked towards the tweens like a panther, eyes narrowed. Then, she pitched forward, bending halfway like a tree in a storm, till she was nose-to-nose with the two rivals. 'You know what I think? I think you two decided to make a bit of pocket money. For the latest video game or fancy phone or whatever you kids are into these days. So, you hatched a sinister plan and stole the nameplates under the cover of darkness. Right?' Her smile was like a chopper knife.

'Wrong!' DJ and Mataji cried out, rising to their feet as fast as their creaky knees would allow. Roshanara and Gajodhar tried to calm them down.

The cop leaned forward menacingly. 'Want to see what a jail looks like from the inside, haan?'

Suraiya quivered with indignation.

Divumber quaked like a building during an earthquake.

Shivers ran down the street's spine.

Without warning, the cop exploded into shrieks of laughter. 'Just joking!'

Suraiya gritted her teeth. Divumber went limp with relief.

The policewoman whipped around, pointing her wand at the staff members. 'One of you is a first-rate criminal. One of us is a first-rate inspector. First and last warning to the culprit. Come forward and surrender.'

The street held its breath. Not one hand went up. Not one person went forward feet. Not one person surrendered.

'It's not the staff,' objected DJ. 'I can vouch for them.' Roshanara and the rest of the staff whew-ed silently.

'My staff's been with me for years,' protested Mataji. 'I trust them with my life.' Gajodhar and the rest of the staff let out a phew of relief.

Chulbul beckoned a hawaldar over. 'Pull up the CCTV footage. Front door and back door.'

The grandparents turned cherry red.

The inspector raised an eyebrow. 'You *do* have CCTV cameras?'

The senior citizens nodded, pointing at the machines outside the restaurant.

The tweens sighed in relief. The footage would reveal the culprit. The culprit would return the priceless treasures. And they'd all go home happy.

'We *do* have CCTV cameras...'

'...but they don't work.'

The cop stared at them dumbfounded. 'Meaning?'

'They're dummy pieces,' said Mataji.

'The real ones were too expensive,' said DJ.

The cop sank into a chair. 'You thought the dummies would scare away potential criminals?'

The senior citizens nodded sheepishly.

Two tween hearts broke for the second time that morning.

'All dismissed!' the cop bellowed like an army sergeant. 'Family meeting.'

She waited till Roshanara and Gajodhar herded the staff away. Then, the policewoman shifted closer to them, holding on to the chair she was seated in, hopping like an energetic bunny. HOPHOPHOPHOPHOP!

When she was at whispering distance, the cop lowered her voice. 'Your nameplates, what are they priced at? Approximately? Rough value? If you were to sell it in the market, how much would it fetch?'

'They're invaluable!' said Suraiya indignantly.

'P-priceless,' stammered Divumber. You couldn't put a price on history, now could you?

'There's a price for everything,' Inspector Chulbul scratched her palm, giving them a meaningful look.

DJ-Suraiya and Divumber-Mataji exchanged horrified looks. Was she asking for a *bribe*?

'Ten per cent discount at our restaurant any time you visit,' Suraiya offered, before Chulbul could quote an astronomical amount.

'Same. Plus, free home delivery,' Divumber matched the offer.

'Lifetime free meal at our restaurant?' proposed Suraiya, when the cop didn't reply.

'For you and your family?' said Divumber frantically.

'KHAMOSH! SILENCE!' Chulbul roared, making everyone jump out of their skins.

'We'll let you talk,' said Divumber meekly.

'Please tell us what you want,' said Suraiya stiffly.

'All I want is the recipe for the Pasinabad Pulao.'

They recoiled.

'I love having people over, love feeding family and friends, serving a lavish feast.' She waved the danda and bottle about like a hospitable host. 'But my pulao never turns out quite like yours.'

All this while, Suraiya and Divumber had hated each other. Suddenly, evil had a new face.

It was daylight robbery! The recipe was a well-kept secret held over generations. A family heirloom. Their grandparents would never share it. Ever.

It was only the sight of the danda and the threat of jail that kept them quiet.

'Okay,' the grandparents chorused defeatedly, before Suraiya and Divumber could protest in horror.

The inspector sprang up and flicked her danda over her head in a Monkey Style Kung Fu move. SWISH! SWISH! SWOOSH! 'Done! I shall apply direct heat on both ends—exactly how you do in the dum style of cooking—and smoke the thief out. Culprit, beware! You can't escape the long arms of...'

'The law,' muttered Suraiya.

'Inspector Chulbul,' finished the cop.

'And the law,' murmured Divumber.

'But mainly, Inspector Chulbul.' She had the last word.

15

When Life Gives You Lemons, Make Lemonade

LATER THAT AFTERNOON, DIVUMBER WAS waiting in the abandoned cinema hall, when Suraiya trudged inside.

'Working together is a bad idea,' began Divumber.

'But the plaques are gone,' finished Suraiya.

'Another joint attack.'

'So, we must join forces.'

'To save our restaurants' legacy.'

'And the Pasinabad Pulao recipe.'

Divumber and Suraiya flopped down on the stage.

'But what if our grandparents give the recipe to Chulbul?' said Divumber worriedly. 'What if she starts her own restaurant? She'll threaten to throw people in jail if they don't eat there. What'll we do then?'

A determined look came into Suraiya's eyes. 'We have to find the plaques ourselves. Before Chulbul does. That's the only way we can keep our recipe and our legacy safe.'

Divumber nodded glumly. 'But how?'

'Let's see what we know.' Suraiya brought out her glittery notebook.

'You've come prepared.' Divumber slipped a hand inside his rucksack and brought out a tin of fruit-flavoured candy. He held it out.

'So have you,' remarked Suraiya, plucking an orange-flavoured one.

Divumber popped a strawberry-flavoured candy into his mouth. 'Let's start with who saw the plaque last?'

'The same person who locked the restaurant. It's usually DJ. But last night, we had to leave early for a Walima,' she jotted down.

'We had to go for a wedding reception, too.' No surprises there. It was wedding season and every day a record number of marriages took place all over town. Local weddings. Destination weddings. Celebrity weddings at the Pasinabad Palace.

'Roshanara was in charge of closing down.'

'Gajodhar locked up the restaurant last night, too.'

Suraiya frowned as something occurred to her. 'Wait a minute, it was Roshanara who recommended the menu printer.'

'And it was Gajodhar who suggested the signboard company,' Divumber squealed.

Suraiya shifted uncomfortably. Could Chulbul be right? Could it be an inside job? All signs pointed to the Head Chefs. *No! Roshanara was her cousin*, she thought loyally. But didn't Ammi always say 'anyone's capable of anything'?

'Maybe Roshanara and Gajodhar are in cahoots,' Suraiya said reluctantly.

Divumber scratched his head. 'What would our Head Chefs even do with the plaques?'

'Put them up at home? Sell them and make a fortune?' She paused. 'And where do people sell ancient things? In an antique shop.'

'But which one? There must be thousands of them in Pasinabad. We're talking about Pasinabad, after all. Wish I could've asked Mataji. If only we could ask someone wise and kind.'

Wise and kind. Suraiya's face lit up. 'There *is* someone we can talk to.'

'Great!' Divumber hesitated. Then, cleared his throat. 'About our Head Chefs. I-I don't know. You heard the grandparents. They said they've known their staff for years.'

Suraiya crossed her arms over her chest. 'Can you really know someone? Take my health conscious-say-no-to-junk-food Ammi, for instance. I caught her red-handed in the kitchen once.' She proceeded to share the story of the Double ka Meetha.

'Must've been really good Double ka Meetha,' remarked Divumber when she reached the end of the tale.

'It was.'

'But—'

'Ha! "But" is the word we use just before making an excuse,' Suraiya cut in, quoting Ammi, sounding exactly like her.

'Mataji said she trusts her staff with her life.' Divumber dropped the 'but', but not the point he was trying to make.

'Trust is like an egg. It's easily broken,' Suraiya said sagely.

A thoughtful look came over Divumber's face. 'I know what you mean,' he said, at last. 'Last year, I put Papa in charge of my Halloween loot. And guess what? He was actually stealing my chocolates behind my back.'

'If he was doing it behind your back, how did you even know?'

'From the zits on his face,' Divumber explained. Papa could never have chocolate without breaking into pimples.

Suraiya gave him a sidelong glance. He'd make a good detective, she thought. Not as good as her, obviously. But still.

Another possibility came to her. 'What if Roshanara and Gajodhar are working *for* Badke Bhaiya?'

Divumber's face clouded over. 'What if our Head Chefs are innocent?'

'What if they aren't?'

'I don't want to hurt them.'

'We won't,' Suraiya assured him. 'Unless they are guilty.'

'I think we should talk to our grandparents.'

'No point,' argued Suraiya. 'They think the world of their chefs.'

'We could turn Gajodhar and Roshanara over to the—'

'Don't say poli—'

'Police.'

'That paan-chewing police is after the Pasinabad Pulao—' Suraiya broke off mid-sentence. Paan! Paan stains! Those weren't blood stains on the restaurant's entrance wall! It was betel juice! She gasped. 'What if Chulbul stole the plaques? Because she wants the recipe so bad?'

Divumber's eyes were round. 'Like ransom? To return them in exchange for the recipe?'

Suraiya brought out her notebook and began to put down all the 'facts' of the case, with Divumber raising objections:

CRIME: THEFT OF THE NAWAB'S PLAQUES

'Shouldn't that be our ancestors' plaques?'

'I'm the one making notes. I'll decide,' Suraiya retorted.

Prime suspects:

1a. Roshanara

1b. Gajodhar

2. Inspector Chulbul

3. Badke Bhaiya

Motive

Roshanara - Gajodhar: Thirst for money

Inspector Chulbul: Hunger for Pasinabad Pulao recipe

Badke Bhaiya: To arm-twist us into shutting shop

'Could be a burglary, if you ask me.'

'No one's asking you.'

Clues

Roshanara - Gajodhar: Had the keys to the restaurants

Inspector Chulbul: Paan stains on restaurant's entrance wall

Badke Bhaiya: His own words

As Suraiya flipped a page, the small, shiny silvery strip showed up.

Divumber picked it up. 'What's this?'

Suraiya shrugged. 'It fell out of the wonky menu. Could be a clue.'

Divumber remembered something. He dug into his rucksack and produced the soft, fluffy, pink ball. 'From the signboard office. Is this a craft pom-pom?'

Suraiya peered at it. 'Could be a clue.' She tucked it carefully inside her notebook and shut it with a *thwop*! Then, she took out the emergency phone from her backpack and dialled a number. 'Hello! Tangewali Bhabhi? Just calling to check...okay, great!...oh, and, one more thing, *please* don't tell Dada Jaan. Will tell him later. Okay? Thanks.'

'You've got a phone?' Divumber gaped.

'Emergency phone. For emergencies only.'

'Your parents gave you a phone?' Divumber just couldn't believe it.

'Parent. It's just me and Ammi.'

'Same pinch, no back pinch. I live with my Papa.'

'How's that the same thing?' she argued.

'I mean, a one parent, one kid.'

'Hardly the same thing.'

Divumber pouted. Working with her was going to be a *task*.

'Well, do you want my number or not?'

Divumber thrust his hand forward.

Suraiya gave him a look. 'Really?'

'Unless you want to tear a page from your precious notebook,' he replied cheekily.

Suraiya huffed.

'That's what I thought,' Divumber gloated as she jotted down her number on his hand.

'Here's Mataji's landline number.'

She gaped at him.

'You know, landline? The phone that doesn't go anywhere?'

'Like this conversation,' grumped Suraiya.

'Mataji's mobile phone is passcode protected,' he said defensively.

'The important thing is,' she said slowly, 'is it Divumber protected?'

'You mean, I should crack the code?'

Suraiya's eyes gleamed. 'I could help you. It's what I want to do when I grow up.'

'You want to crack codes and rob banks?'

'The term is Systems Software Specialist,' she informed him with a superior smile. 'SSS.'

'So, you *do* want to become a bank robber!'

Suraiya rolled her eyes. 'A *hacker*. The good kind. They do the wrong things for the right reasons.'

'I bet that's what Badke Bhaiya tells himself,' retorted Divumber.

'What do *you* want to do when you grow up?'

Divumber puffed up like a poori. 'Neta. Foreign tours. Beacon light cars. Long speeches.'

Suraiya stared at him, speechless.

16

Walking on Eggshells

'WHERE TO?' ASKED DIVUMBER AS they stepped out of Fillum Talkies.

'Chowk intersection,' replied Suraiya.

It was time to talk to someone wise and wonderful.

They ducked and weaved through the narrow gully, emerging at the next street. Where a Tangewali Bhabhi was waiting for them.

***

'There's no one else we can turn to, Gullu Didi,' Suraiya beseeched, recounting the entire story. 'Please help, Didi.'

Seconds ticked by. Eyes blinked. Lips moved, but no sound came out. At last, Gullu Didi dabbed the edge of her moist eyes with her saree pallu. 'You've chosen to trust me? A complete stranger?'

'You're not a stranger,' protested Suraiya. Their paths had literally crossed every single day.

Gullu Didi covered her mouth and nose with both hands. 'I-I don't know what to say,' her voice cracked.

'You could tell us the name of the best antique shop in Pasinabad,' said Divumber impatiently. 'Oww!' he yelped as Suraiya poked him in the ribs.

The two newfound partners were standing on a footpath near the smoggy Chowk junction with a foggy-eyed Gullu Didi.

'Purana Maal,' said Gullu Didi. 'It's the oldest antique shop in Pasinabad. Talk to the owner. He knows everything there is to know about antiques. Must be as old as your grandparents, if not older. Tell him Gullu sends her regards.'

Suraiya scribbled down the details in her notebook.

Divumber glanced up at the clock tower and squealed, 'Is that the time? We better rush back.'

'Let's go to Purana Maal tomorrow.' Suraiya turned to Gullu Didi. 'Don't know how to thank you, Didi.'

'No thanks needed.' She placed a hand of blessing on Suraiya's head. 'Bas, make it quick. The thief is sure to try and sell the bronze plaques at the Machli Gala this weekend.'

Goosebumps sprouted on two pairs of tween hands. 'How can you be so sure?'

'Because the biggest antique smuggler in town is going to be there.'

'Who?' Suraiya and Divumber clamoured.

Gullu Didi lowered her voice. 'Hullad Sirji.'

Divumber's tummy twisted. 'The Chief Guest at the Machli Gala?'

Suraiya's heart hammered. 'The one who's standing for elections this year?'

They'd seen his posters. They'd seen him on the news. It was all anyone could talk about in their restaurants. In all of

Pasinabad, for that matter. Hullad Sirji was the talk of the town.

Two tween heads reeled. First crooked businessman, then cunning cop, now corrupt neta. They were entangled in a mystery twistier than a jalebi.

'Is there no one we can trust?' Divumber cried, dismayed.

'You can trust each other,' said Gullu Didi solemnly, placing her arms on their shoulders.

Divumber and Suraiya exchanged a glance. Looked like they had no choice.

'What do we do now?'

'Let's not rush into anything. Let's think with a calm and cool head,' Suraiya replied, feeling uncalm, her head uncool.

***

'What's up, buddy? You look stressed,' asked Papa.

Divumber had borrowed Mataji's phone to video-call Papa. All this while he'd chatted normally because he didn't want to stress Papa out. But as Papa stroked the phone screen as if to soothe his stress away, the words spilled out of him. 'It's just been one mystery after another.'

'What mystery?' asked Papa curiously.

'Like the Nimona Lajawaab...'

To Divumber's surprise, Papa's cheeks turned a pretty shade of pink.

'You know something about it?!'

'No, no. Not at all. Why would you think that?'

'Papa!' Divumber waggled a finger. 'I know you.'

Papa tried to wiggle his way out of it, but Divumber was like a stubborn crocodile. In the end, he dragged it out of Papa.

'That's it?' pooh-poohed Divumber, after Papa recounted the whole story. 'That's no reason to think a dish is cursed.' Papa smiled sheepishly.

***

'Are you *sure* no one's tried to sell it to you?' asked Suraiya.

Mr Purana Maal cocked his head to one side. 'If someone tried to sell me a historical artefact, I'd notice. Trust me.'

It was the next afternoon. Heeding Gullu Didi's advice, they'd landed up at Purana Maal. The antique store was in Chor Bazaar, a noisy, distant, congested part of town. They'd never been here before. And after this visit, they doubted they'd ever be back.

'So, you haven't seen anything that looked like this in the last few days? Please try and remember.' Divumber enlarged the plaque's photos on Suraiya's phone. Luckily, she'd clicked lots and lots of photos on her first day in Pasinabad.

Mr Purana Maal gave him a withering look. 'A plaque bestowed by Nawab Naak-Mein-Dum would be pretty hard to forget.'

Suraiya and Divumber were crushed. They'd reached yet another dead end.

'At least tell us the price of the bronze plaque?' pleaded Suraiya, thinking on her feet. 'Approximately? Rough value?'

Mr Purana Maal exhaled in exasperation. 'That's something only Daddy-ji would be able to help with.'

Suraiya and Divumber looked around hopefully.

'Daddy-ji's frail and feeble and laid up in bed. He hasn't been to the shop in ages.'

Someone sniffled. Later, Suraiya would claim it was Divumber. Divumber would insist it was Suraiya.

'Tell you what,' said Mr. Purana Maal, his heart melting. 'Daddy-ji keeps a logbook. It has the price list of all the priceless artefacts he's ever sold or bought. If there's another item from the Nawab Naak-Mein-Dum's times, we might just get a ballpark figure. Let me see if I can find it.'

'We'll wait right here.'

'Thanks so much.'

As the antique dealer disappeared behind a curtain, the two tweens browsed around the shop.

Divumber picked up a toothbrush that looked more like a broomstick, ignoring the '*Once-broken-consider-it-sold*' sign. 'Look! Nawab Naak-Mein-Dum's toothbrush.' Grabbing a brass magnifying glass, Divumber continued the dental inspection. 'I spy with my antique eye, royal plaque.'

Suraiya giggled.

'This isn't the logbook I was talking about.' Mr Purana Maal came back, muttering to himself. As he flipped through the pages of the ledger, a black-and-white photo slipped out of it. Lost in thought, the antique shop owner walked away without noticing it.

In a flash, Divumber swooped down, picked up the photo and opened his mouth to call the owner back. That's when he noticed something. He stared and stared at the photo in fascination. Then, he quickly stuffed it inside his shirt.

Suraiya gawped. He seemed to have taken the name Chor Bazaar very seriously! 'What are you doing?' she hissed.

Before Divumber could reply, light footsteps sounded.

The tweens tried to look as innocent as possible.

'I'm afraid I couldn't find the logbook. Will keep looking around and call you if I find something. Could you please forward the photo of the plaque? Here's my number.'

Thanking Mr Purana Maal profusely, Suraiya and Divumber took their leave.

'What's wrong with you?' Suraiya scolded as soon as they were at a safe distance. 'How could you steal that photo?'

He pulled her to one side and brought it out. 'Look,' he pointed. He tried to enlarge the photo, before remembering it wasn't a picture on a phone.

'What exactly am I looking at?' She peered at the photo of two strapping young men smiling at the camera.

The one on the left looked exactly like Mr Purana Maal. 'Must be Senior Mr Purana Maal,' remarked Suraiya.

Divumber pointed at the other.

'Do you know who he's standing next to?' He answered his own query. 'How would you know? You've never met my Dadaji.'

Suraiya plucked it from Divumber's hand and felt around the edges.

Her fingers snagged on something. 'Wait, what's this? Let me see—' he broke off, bewildered. The photo had been neatly folded into two.

There were two more young men, standing next to Senior Mr Purana Maal and Divumber's Dadaji.

Suraiya released the flap and her jaw dropped. 'Our grandfathers were friends?' she asked in a strangled voice.

'*What*?' Divumber squinted at the photo. 'Which one's your grandpa?'

She pointed to the third friend, the one standing right next to Divumber's Dadaji. 'That's Dada Jaan.' Reaching for her phone, she quietly clicked a photo of the photograph.

'Our grandparents. Friends.' Divumber sounded dazed. 'My Dadaji–Mataji and your Dada Jaan–Dadi Jaan must've had a huge fight.'

Suraiya hmm-ed. 'Because of the Nimona Lajawaab?'

'Maybe that's why they stopped talking to each other?'

'That seems to be the only logical explanation.'

Divumber stared at the photo again. 'Who's that?' he pointed at the fourth friend.

Suraiya scrutinized the photo. In vain. Though the young man looked awfully familiar, they couldn't really place him.

The two walked on, their heads spinning faster than the blades of the ceiling fan in summer. And what they saw next made their heads spin faster than a washing machine on the fastest setting.

Right across from them were Roshanara and Gajodhar, clutching newspaper cones, tossing roasted chana into their mouths, giggling like buddies, as they strolled down the street.

17

Half a Loaf Is Better than None

DIVUMBER RUBBED HIS EYES. 'DID we just see...? Was it really...?'

'Oh, yes,' Suraiya confirmed, a steely look in her eyes.

'They're friends? Since when?' Divumber said in a strangled voice.

'But Roshanara hasn't been out of my sight...' Suraiya trailed off. Except every afternoon! Breath of fresh air indeed. So, this is where she disappeared off to every day.

'Suspicion confirmed. They ganged up and stole the plaques,' Divumber exclaimed. 'Let's go and confront them right now—'

'You think they'll confess?' Suraiya held him back. 'No. We need to stop it.'

'Stop our Head Chefs from meeting each other?'

'No, silly. Think about it. They have the plaques, so why haven't they skipped town yet?'

'Maybe they're working for Badke Bhaiya?' Divumber guessed. 'Maybe they've already handed the plaques to him?'

'Maybe. But remember what Gullu Didi said? The thief will sell the plaques to Hullad Sirji. At the Machli Gala. Tomorrow evening. We need to stop the *sale* from happening.'

Divumber's eyes widened. 'You mean gate crash? Sneak into a high-profile, heavily guarded event? Impossible! It'd be easier to travel to Mars and return by the weekend. Didn't you see the card? Strictly by invitation. How'd we even get in?'

'Whoever said anything about sneaking in?' She pointed at the giggling Head Chefs and gave Divumber an expectant look.

He let out a sweetly sinister laugh, catching on.

***

'So, all set for the Machli Gala?' Divumber followed Gajodhar into the pantry, the next evening.

The Head Bawarchi preened, reaching for the almond gunny sack. 'I'm rushing home soon to get ready.'

'What you wearing?'

'Designer outfit.'

'Same,' Divumber dimpled.

'Dreaming in daylight?' Gajodhar gloated. 'Only two people from the restaurant are going to the Machli Gala. Mataji and me.'

Divumber's eyes glinted. 'You mean, Mataji and *me*. Because you're down with loosies.' He leaned forward, lowering his voice, 'All that roasted chana you ate.'

Gajodhar's face blanched. 'W-w-what?'

'Forgot your little picnic at Chor Bazaar? Last afternoon?'

The chef looked paler than the leaves of a malnourished bamboo plant.

'Ha!' Divumber smirked. 'I'll tell Mataji that you had to rush home. That I'm going to the Machli Gala in your place.'

'Listen to me,' bleated the chef, 'I can explain—'

'Thank you for lending me your phone and earphones.' Divumber plucked them out of Gajodhar's pocket. 'See you tomorrow morning.' With that, Divumber slammed the pantry door shut, locked it and dropped the key in his pocket.

***

'One more, just one more,' coaxed Dada Jaan, clicking Suraiya's photo.

'Last one,' she grumbled, fidgeting with the dupatta of her stunning, scratchy pink gharara.

Roshanara had come down with a stomach bug. (After Suraiya had brought up the roasted chana and the Chor Bazaar excursion, of course.) And here she was now, at the Machli Gala with Dada Jaan. It was held at the majestic, awe-inspiring, painstakingly-restored Pasinabad Palace every year.

The Concert Hall left Suraiya awestruck. The high-ceilings, gilded chandeliers, vintage carpets and antique furniture screamed royal splendour. Celebrity chefs posed for selfies and signed notebooks, napkins, plaster casts and foreheads of screaming fans. Guests in sequinned sarees, shimmering shararas, designer dhotis and shiny sherwanis bustled around the hall. Servers sporting white uniforms and colourful turbans, zoomed around on roller skates, plying guests with mouth-watering Mutton Seekh, tongue-tingling Tunde Ke Kebab, lip-smacking Litchi Sherbet, palate-pleasing Panna and more.

'Look, there's Chef Ramsay.' DJ spotted a familiar face in the crowd.

Suraiya's head whipped around in excitement. 'Gordon Ramsay?'

'Gogo Ramsay,' DJ corrected. 'He's world-famous in Pasinabad. And there's Chef O'Lever.'

'Jamie Oliver?' squealed Suraiya.

'Jimmy O'Lever. His Murgh Pasanda is to cry for.'

'You mean "to die for", DJ.'

'Tauba, why should anyone die for Murgh Pasanda? Crying happy tears is better, hai na?'

Suraiya tapped her foot impatiently. She really needed to go look for Divumber and put their plan into motion. 'When will the programme begin, DJ?'

'Can a programme begin without the Chief Guest? Hullad Sirji should be here soon. Why don't you look around, soak up some culture? But stay away from the bhool bhulaiya, okay? It's impossible to find your way out without a guide.'

Suraiya nodded, waved him goodbye and scurried out of the Concert Hall.

'The name is Bul. Chul-bul,' came a familiar voice.

Suraiya sucked in a breath. The inspector looked almost harmless in a red floral saree, glass bangles, bindi and gajra.

'What are you doing here?' demanded the cop, adjusting her pallu.

'I-uh, was thinking about exploring the bhool bhulaiya,' Suraiya said quickly. 'But it's too risky. They say no one can find their way out without help.'

'Ha! Then, they haven't met me, Chulbul,' the cop boasted. 'Watch, I'll be out of the maze garden like *this*.'

'Oh! You're so brave,' Suraiya cooed in admiration.

'See you in five minutes.' Chulbul hitched up her saree pleats and off she marched to the bhool bhulaiya.

Suraiya dusted her hands. Prime Suspect Two was out of the picture.

***

Back in the Concert Hall, Divumber pretend-groaned. 'I have to go to the washroom.'

'Told you not to drink so much water on the way,' Mataji chided. 'Hurry back. And don't get lost.'

'Don't worry, will call you. I have Gajodhar's phone.' Divumber raced out of the Concert Hall, only to bump into someone.

'We meet again!' A familiar face smirked at him.

For a moment, Divumber didn't recognize him. The don was wearing a wavy wig and a jazzy kurta-pyjama. The Men in Black were still...in black.

'Badke Bhaiya!' A shiver ran down his spine.

Prime Suspect Three had arrived! To sell the plaques to Hullad Sirji!

Divumber ducked behind a pillar, whipped out his phone (that is to say, Gajodhar's phone) and called his partner-in-(solving)-crime.

***

Suraiya's heart hammered as Divumber gave her the news. It was time to swing into action. She hurried towards the washrooms and scanned the area. Where was he? Pressing her earphones, she dialled his number. That is to say, Gajodhar's number.

'Psst! Over here,' whispered a tall, leafy potted plant.

Suraiya looked this way and that, before ducking behind the talking plant.

Divumber was dressed snazzily in a beige kurta-pyjama and red Nehru jacket. A pair of dark glasses and jootis with upturned soles completed his look.

'Where's the, uh,' he broke off to cough, 'weapon?'

She fished out a small envelope out of her potli bag and pressed it into his palm. 'Let's go over the plan one last time—'

A cheer went up in the plush lobby before Suraiya could complete her sentence. 'Hullad Sirji, say cheese, please-ji! Do you have a message for our readers, Sirji?' called out the photographers and journalists.

Mission Stop Sale was a go! Suraiya and Divumber bumped fists. Pressing a finger to their earphones, they turned around and walked back into the Concert Hall, melting into the crowd.

'Any luck?' Suraiya spoke in Divumber's ear, a few minutes later, clutching a glass of Jal Jeera.

He shook his head glumly, balancing a glass of Aam Panna.

'Are you shaking your head?' Suraiya asked crossly. 'I can't see you, you know. You need to speak up.'

'No luck. Haven't been able to get close to Hullad Sirji.'

'Hurryhurryhurry.'

Suraiya and Divumber began moving closer to their target.

'NOW!' shrilled Suraiya as two volunteers hurried up to the soon-to-be neta. She spun around and strode away.

Divumber walked close to Hullad Sir-ji and—DHAAANGGGG— accidentally-on-purpose bumped into him, splooshing him with the Aam Panna. As the drink made an embarrassingly tell-tale stain on his dhoti, Divumber picked up pace and vanished into the throng of guests.

'Abey O!' shouted Volunteer 1.

'Watch it!' yelled Volunteer 2, before whisking the Chief Guest away.

Suraiya tailed them at a safe distance as they hurried towards the washrooms. To her dismay, they ushered him inside, standing guard at the entrance.

Oh, no! How are we going to get rid of the volunteers? Suraiya thought in dismay.

She waited for them to leave, but they refused to budge. Minutes ticked by. Taking a deep breath, she sashayed up to them. 'Excuse me, please? Madam President's looking for you.'

'Madam President? Of the country?' asked Volunteer 1.

Suraiya stared at him. 'Madam President. Of the Machli Committee.'

'Looking for us?' asked Volunteer 2.

Suraiya smiled angelically.

'Why?' Volunteer 1 asked suspiciously.

Suraiya shrugged.

'We're staying right here,' Volunteer 2 said firmly.

'Okay. I hope she doesn't get angry with you.'

The two men gulped, hesitated and *finally* trotted away.

Suraiya was about to call Divumber and tell him the coast was clear when her phone rang. Her pulse raced as she saw the name flashing on the screen.

18

There's No such Thing as a Free Lunch

'UFF!' HULLAD SIRJI MUTTERED UNDER his breath, trying to dry his dhoti with the help of the hand dryer. 'Why can't people see where they're going?' He craned his neck as a flush sounded.

Divumber stepped out of a stall, his face brightening at the sight of the neta. 'Oh, it's you!' he cried, throwing himself on the neta's feet. 'Big fan, Sirji!'

'Hmm,' said the neta, pompously.

'Today's my lucky day, Sirji' Divumber crowed, slipping a hand inside his kurta pocket and whipping out the 'weapon' from the envelope—a twig of Behosh. He was about to make the neta sniff the spice when his phone pinged.

'Mission Stop Sale cancelled,' said Suraiya urgently. 'Don't do it.'

'What? Why?' Divumber squawked. That was the plan, wasn't it? Spill drink on Hullad Sirji. Accost him in the washroom. Knock him out with Behosh. Beat hasty retreat.

The thief could hardly sell the plaques to an unconscious antique smuggler now, could they?

'Mr Purana Maal called. There's been a...new development. Will explain later. Let Hullad Sirji go.'

'Let go!' grunted the neta, as Divumber's hands tightened around his legs. '*What* are you doing?'

'Wait,' hissed Suraiya in Divumber's ear. 'Mr Purana Maal's calling again.'

'Uh-ah-okay,' mumbled Divumber. The leader was struggling like an elephant trying to break free from a crocodile's snappy jaws. Seeing Divumber distracted on a call, Hullad Sirji snatched the herb out of his hand. 'What's this?' He held it up to his nose and took a suspicious sniff. And another.

Divumber watched in horror as Hullad Sirji staggered around the washroom, spinning and crashing into the stall door.

'All okay?' Suraiya whispered through the washroom door. 'I'm coming in!' she hissed, as the Chief Guest fell into a swoon.

'What did you do that for?' she chided, letting herself into the washroom. 'Told you to let him go.'

'I didn't do anything!' Divumber wailed. 'He only snatched, sniffed, fainted.'

Someone banged on the washroom door.

'O Sirji! All okay?' sang a voice.

'It's time for your speech, Sirji,' trilled another.

Suraiya and Divumber exchanged horrified looks. The volunteers were back!

***

The tweens were in a fix. Giving a speech is rather tough when you're unconscious.

'What do we do now?' Suraiya said, panicking.

'I'm thinking,' huffed Divumber, propping the neta against a wall.

'Think faster.'

An idea crawled into Divumber's brain. 'Luckily for us, we have a great speaker in our midst.'

Suraiya held up a hand. 'Please don't say it's you.'

'It's me.'

He told her what he had in mind.

'I don't know...' Suraiya said slowly.

The volunteers thumped on the door again.

Suraiya quickly flashed a thumbs-up.

Holding the door ajar, Divumber peeped out, looking calm, composed and cheerful.

'Hullad Sirji needs five more minutes.'

'Why?' demanded Volunteer 1.

Volunteer 2 stood on tiptoes, trying to peep inside the washroom.

'Because um, he's changing his hairstyle. He, er, wants to look his best tonight,' Divumber said the first thing that came into his head. 'He'll join you at the Concert Hall soon.'

'We'll wait right here.'

Divumber sucked in a breath. 'F-f-fine,' he stammered, , 'b-b-but don't knock again, okay. He's getting annoyed. And you know what happens when he gets annoyed.'

The volunteers gulped. They didn't know and they didn't want to find out.

Divumber was half-afraid they'd force their way inside, but thankfully they turned around reluctantly and walked away.

'All clear,' Divumber told the washroom door.

Suraiya sneaked out, the red Nehru jacket wrapped on her arm. She dashed towards a server, who was hurrying back to the kitchen with an empty platter. She took him aside and made him an offer, holding out the jacket. Suraiya held her breath as the server mulled it over. To her relief, he held out a hand, accepting the jacket and the offer.

***

The Concert Hall erupted into applause as Madam President took the stage. 'Welcome, one and all! On behalf of the Machli Committee, I welcome you to Pasinabad's grandest spectacle of creativity and imagination—the Machli Gala. A magnificent celebration of our history, heritage, cuisine and, of course, the Masterchefs who lovingly preserve and painstakingly recreate the timeless recipes. I now invite our Chief Guest, Hullad Sirji, to share a few nuggets—food pun unintended, ha ha!—of wisdom.'

Madam President gaped as Suraiya and Divumber rolled out the Chief Guest on to the stage. The neta was now wearing a pair of dark glasses, a colourful turban and a pair of roller skates. Suraiya had traded Divumber's jacket for them. The server had walked away, a happy man indeed.

The no-longer-feuding foodies wheeled Hullad Sirji like a trolley with wonky wheels. They didn't dare look at the audience in fear of locking eyes with their grandparents. They couldn't begin to imagine the look on their faces.

As Suraiya steadied the neta in front of the podium, Divumber picked up Madam President's welcome speech that was still lying on the lectern. He held it aloft, covering Hullad Sirji's face.

Suraiya placed her phone down on the lectern and adjusted the height of the microphone. Divumber jabbed the text-to-speech app on her phone, selected a voice effect and began typing furiously. 'Friends, Pasinabadis, countrymen!' Out came a deep, rich, heavy baritone. It sounded a lot like Mataji's favourite actor. The one who hosted the popular quiz show on TV.

Suraiya gave him a little nudge.

Divumber cleared his throat. 'Good evening! Thank you for placing your trust in me and choosing me as your leader.'

Suraiya gave him a not-so-little nudge.

'I mean, choosing me as your Chief Guest. I'd like to thank Madam President and the Machli Committee for inviting me to the Machli Gala...' Divumber was about to type further when the phone's automatic Lock Screen feature played spoilsport and the screen went dark.

As Suraiya leaned forward to assist him, Hullad Sirji's sunglasses slid down his nose. At the same time, the colourful turban began its slow descent from his head, slipping down to his forehead. Battling stubborn technology, silky fabric and a sweaty nose, the two valiantly plodded on.

At the end of the painful (for them and the audience) speech, Suraiya and Divumber handed the responsibility of handling Hullad Sirji to a most bewildered Madam President. Then, they turned around and tore out of the Concert Hall at breakneck speed.

19

Easy as Pie

THEY DASHED OUT INTO THE lobby, past Nawab Naak-Mein-Dum's statue, through the portico, down the marble steps, across the driveway, along the lush landscaped lawns, right up to the gazebo. Their phones pinged as they plopped down, puffing and panting. They didn't need to look at the screens to know it was DJ and Mataji. The elders were calling for answers. As it happened, the friendly-foodies had a few unanswered questions themselves.

Don't worry. Will explain everything later. See you in the portico after dinner—they texted their grandparents.

'Why didn't you want me to knock out Hullad Sirji?' panted Divumber.

'Badke Bhaiya couldn't have sold him the plaques,' she replied quietly.

'What? Why?'

'Because any antique dealer would've told him the truth.'

'Which is?'

'You can't sell a fake.'

'Your plaque's fake?'

Suraiya scowled. Divumber was acting like a Squelchy Shallot all over again.

'*Both* our plaques are.'

Divumber went still. 'There must be some mistake—'

'Mr Purana Maal said so. He found his father's logbook earlier today.'

'The one with the price list of everything they'd ever bought and sold?' asked Divumber, wiping his sweaty forehead with the back of his hand.

'And *made*,' Suraiya exhaled. 'At the request of his friends.'

'Our grandparents requested Senior Mr Purana Maal to *make* fakes?'

She nodded grimly, fanning herself with the zari-trimmed dupatta.

'If the plaques are fake,' Divumber couldn't bring himself to believe it, 'why did our grandparents report the theft to the cops?'

'They didn't,' Suraiya pointed out. 'It was the Head Bawarchis and the rest of us at the restaurant. Think about it.'

'Uff! It's too hot to think.' Divumber brought a pouch of mouth freshener from his kurta pocket, tore it open and emptied the contents into his mouth.

Suraiya went still. A scene flashed in front of her eyes. She bent forward and picked up the torn piece of foil. And another missing piece of the jigsaw fell into place.

'Know anyone who's good at calligraphy?' she asked Divumber, on a hunch.

'Good? I know an expert. That's why I didn't sign up for a course...'

Suraiya's eyes widened when he shared the name. The knotted mystery began to unravel, one knot at a time. Could it really be? No! It couldn't. And yet, it all added up. Everything pointed to it.

'Let's see the photo you flicked again—'

'—borrowed,' he corrected, '*borrowed* from Mr Purana Maal's shop.'

Suraiya rolled her eyes, scrolling through her phone till she found what she was looking for.

She enlarged the black-and-white photo and inspected it from all angles. Four friends. Senior Mr Purana Maal. Divumber's Dadaji. Suraiya's Dada Jaan. And a familiar stranger. 'What are we missing?'

'Wait a minute! What if the fourth friend was missing hair?' Divumber covered his hair (not his own, the fourth friend's) with a hand. 'Doesn't he...' His voice rose in excitement. '....he does look like...?'

'It *is* him!' Suraiya squawked.

The final piece of the puzzle fell into place with a satisfying *click*. They looked at each other, hearts thumping, mouths dry.

'Quick. We need to call a Tangewali Bhabhi.'

'Why?

'Because we need a ride back to the restaurants, Divumber.'

'Restaurants? Have you seen the time, Suraiya? It'll be closing time soon.'

'Then, hurry! We know who stole the plaques. And it's time someone else knows it, too.'

***

Suraiya had heard stories of infamous chefs and their foul tempers. Throwing pans at the wall. Smashing plates. Breaking ladles like they were breadsticks. Karate-chopping chopping boards. When DJ entered Shaan-e-Daawat half an hour later, he looked like he was about to do all the above.

Suraiya rose from a table, gulping. She'd never seen this side of her grandpa.

'You left without telling me and came all the way to the restaurant. At night. All alone. Do you have any idea how dangerous it could've been, mohtarma?'

Mohtarma. Young lady. Not Suraiya. He was *that* mad at her.

'I'm so sorry, DJ. I texted you before I left. A Tangewali Bhabhi dropped me. And I wasn't alone.'

'...and don't even get me started on the stunt you pulled with Hullad Sirji.'

Suraiya felt a pang of regret. 'It was an accident. Is he going to be okay?'

'He's going to be fine.' DJ glowered at her. 'He'd come around when I left the palace. A bit groggy and dazed, but that's to be expected.'

She walked up to him slowly and wrapped her arms around his waist.

DJ, who was boiling like a cauldron of water, seemed to cool down a bit. 'Do you know how worried I was? Never ever do that again,' he scolded, squeezing her tight.

'Never ever,' she promised, breathing shakily into his kurta.

'There better be a good explanation for this.'

‘DJ, we did the wrong thing for the right reason,’ said Suraiya, and gave someone a missed call.

As the door flew open, DJ’s mouth dropped open. Divumber ushered a red-faced Mataji in.

20

You Can't Make an Omelette Without Breaking Some Eggs

THE TWO SENIORS DIDN'T BOTHER looking at each other as Mataji sat across the table from DJ.

Divumber cleared his throat. 'Sorry, we didn't mean to worry you. But we know.'

'Know what?' asked Mataji warily.

'We know who stole the plaques,' said Suraiya.

'Who?' demanded DJ.

'Why don't we show you?' offered Divumber gently.

'Turn that way, please,' Suraiya instructed.

'The culprits are there,' the two of them chorused as the grandparents turned towards the gilt-edged mirror on the wall.

Their eyes widened in shock.

Suraiya turned to Dada Jaan and gave him the small, shiny, silvery piece of foil. 'The torn bit of your supari pouch.'

'I believe this belongs to you.' Divumber handed Mataji the colourful pom-pom, pointing at the pink tassels of her saree pallu, 'Madam Calligraphy Expert.'

Divumber spoke in his most leader-like voice. 'We know you stole the plaques.'

'Dhattt!' scoffed DJ.

'How can you steal something that belongs to you?' asked Mataji acerbically.

'Fine. You made them disappear. There, does that sound better?' said Suraiya soothingly, like she was talking to cranky babies.

DJ crossed his arms over his chest. 'Why would we do something like that?'

'Because the plaques are fake!' the tweens said in unison.

DJ cringed. Mataji winced.

'Because you were worried that the truth would come out someday,' said Divumber quietly. 'That someone would find out. And your restaurant's reputation, its legacy would suffer. And that's why, you decided to join hands and bury the past.'

Suraiya brought her hands down on the table loudly. 'And together, you staged a string of disruptive acts. The wonky menu. The awful signboard. The rotten reviews. They were all part of your elaborate plan. To make it look like someone was out to sabotage the restaurants.'

'So that when you finally stole...erm... made the plaques disappear, no one would suspect you,' Divumber said.

A smug look came over Suraiya's face. 'No one except us.'

Divumber puffed out his chest. 'We went behind your back. Joined forces. Sniffed out clues, drew up a list of likely suspects, went after every lead. And after a few wrong turns, our nose led us directly to you.'

'Oh, you both were good. But not as good as us.' Suraiya patted herself on the back.

She scrolled through her phone till she reached the photo of the four friends. Placing the phone on the table, she slid it towards the seniors. 'Dada Jaan. Divumber's Dada-ji. Senior Mr Purana Maal. And last but not least, *Badke Bhaiya.*'

'He had a thick head of hair back then,' observed Divumber astutely. 'Got your best friend to stage a little play, didn't you? Phoolo and Saad. That's what he'd called you the day he dropped by. It was a slip of the tongue. But nothing gets past us. *Nothing.*'

Suraiya took over. 'Badke Bhaiya doesn't want to evict you. He doesn't want to build a food court here. He was only following your orders. You wanted to lead everyone on a wild goose chase. You wanted to create chaos. You wanted everyone to feel sorry for you. So that no one would suspect you when you made the plaques vanish.'

The restaurant was so quiet, you could hear a tablecloth drop.

DJ put his head down on the table. Mataji buried her face in her hands. Soon, their shoulders started shaking uncontrollably.

'Mataji?'

'DJ?'

DJ lifted his head, grinning. Mataji peeked through her fingers.

'Tastes good, doesn't it?' DJ asked, eyes twinkling with mischief.

Suraiya and Divumber looked bewildered. 'What?'

'Peace Pulao,' replied Mataji, her eyes dancing with merriment.

Suraiya and Divumber were gobsmacked.

'You mean...?'

'Are you saying...?'

The grandparents grinned.

'You *planned* this ruse so we'd join hands?'

'You *wanted* us to become friends?'

DJ beamed. 'Did you hear that, Phoolo? They're friends now.'

'I did, Saad, I did. They're friends. Just like we used to be.'

Suraiya and Divumber plonked down on the table, their minds whirling with questions, doubts, unsolved mysteries.

'And here I thought the cursed dish was one big mystery,' said Suraiya.

'No mystery there,' said Divumber, recalling the conversation he'd had with his father. 'Papa had learned how to make the Nimona Lajawaab from a famous Ustad in Pasinabad. It was a long, long time ago. When Papa was young. But something went wrong, I don't know what exactly. I guess they had a fight or something? Papa said things got so complicated, he stopped making the dish altogether.'

Suraiya glowered at him. 'You're telling me this *now*?' She gasped as something occurred to her. 'Ustad Saadat.'

Divumber shot her a puzzled look. 'Who?'

'Dada Jaan. He used to be a celebrated chef, many many *many* years ago, when he was young.'

DJ rolled his eyes at the many manys.

'And Nimona Lajawaab was his signature dish.'

'You're telling me this *now*?' Divumber squeaked. 'So, your DJ taught my Papa how to make the Nimona Lajawaab?'

Suraiya nodded.

'But what happened? Why did the families stop talking to each other?' A horrifying thought flitted into Divumber's mind. 'Wait, you don't think Papa stole the recipe? He'd never!'

'That's what I thought. In the beginning. But that's not it. Something doesn't add up.' The puzzle niggled away in Suraiya's mind. Complicated. A long time ago. Where had she heard the exact same words before? She sat up straight as it hit her. 'When did your Papa move to the city?'

'In 2013. Exactly a year before he adopted me.'

'Same. Ammi left Pasinabad in 2013. Adopted me in 2014.'

Divumber's eyes widened.

'When was the last time your Papa visited Pasinabad?'

'After moving away? Never. This is my first trip here. Imagine!'

'Same. And your Papa never got married.'

'Yes. How did you know?'

'Because neither did Ammi.'

Suraiya's brain whirred. What had Ammi said...yes, that Dada Jaan didn't approve! She turned to the seniors. 'When did you find out? The exact date?'

'Find out what?' asked DJ gently.

'That his Papa and my Ammi wanted to get married?'

Divumber's jaw dropped.

'The last day of October,' replied Mataji, her eyes brimming with unshed tears. 'I remember it like it was yesterday.'

'Tell them from the beginning, Phoolo.'

'Swayam and Ghazal were back from America after finishing college,' Mataji sniffled. 'Swayam wanted to learn a special recipe. And your Dada Jaan—the great Ustad Saadat—graciously agreed to teach him.'

DJ dabbed his eyes. 'They were childhood friends. They lost touch when they went to America to study. Because of the Nimona Lajawaab, they got to spend a lot of time together in the kitchen. The next thing we knew, they wanted to get married to each other—'

'—we were horrified. Friendship's one thing. But love? Marriage? Inter-faith marriage?'

'Phoolo and I had a huge row. We stopped talking to each other. I never made Nimona Lajawaab again. I thought it was manhoos, cursed.'

A heavy silence settled on the restaurant.

'How can love be the reason to hate?' Divumber tasted a tear.

'I wish food could be everyone's faith.' Suraiya swallowed a sob.

21

Best Thing Since Sliced Bread

MATAJI AND DJ HUNG THEIR heads down.

'We were wrong, *so* wrong.'

'Swayam and Ghazal were heartbroken. They moved to two different cities. Never came back. Never got married. Never let their children visit their hometown.'

'And years later, we saw our grandchildren become angry and bitter and go down the same path of hate,' murmured DJ. He held up a hand. 'Don't ask how we knew about your enmity.'

'We have eyes and ears everywhere,' Mataji asserted.

Divumber wondered if their grandparents had overheard the staff discussing their loud fights. Suraiya wondered if the dummy CCTVs were actual dummies.

Mataji smiled through her tears. 'That's when we realized there was only one way to stop the hate.'

'That's when you got together and hatched the plan,' Suraiya snivelled. 'You were willing to go that far?'

'You nearly destroyed the legacy of the restaurants,' Divumber snuffled.

'*You*, our grandchildren, are our legacy.'

'What kind of grandparents would we be if we let you make the same mistake?'

Suraiya and Divumber looked at each other.

'We could've been family,' Suraiya said in wonder.

'You certainly fight like siblings,' remarked Mataji, stroking Suraiya's head. Suraiya threw her arms around Mataji and buried her nose in her saree.

'From family friends to feuding families to family,' smiled DJ, hugging Divumber close. 'Shaan-e-Daawat finally feels like a *family* restaurant.'

They stayed that way for heaven knows how long.

Divumber wiped his nose at long last. 'Do you still have the plaques?'

'I think I know where they are,' said Suraiya quietly, getting to her feet.

She walked up to the heavy safe in the reception area and punched the six-digit passcode. The day the Nimona Lajawaab came between the families. 31-12-13. The door swung open. Sure enough, the historical artefact was lying there in all its Nawabi glory.

'So that's where you've hidden it.' Divumber waggled a finger at Mataji.

'So grateful everything's sorted,' said the seniors after another round of tears and hugging.

'Not everything,' said Divumber.

'Our parents won't ever come to Pasinabad,' said Suraiya.

DJ and Mataji exchanged a look. 'But we know exactly how to sort that out!' they said in unison.

'Don't tell us anything,' DJ put his hands up, leaning back.

Mataji agreed. 'So, when your parents ask us, we can deny any knowledge of the plan.'

Suraiya turned to Divumber, fishing out a key from her potli. 'But first, we need to rescue someone from the pantry.'

Divumber smacked his forehead. 'The Head Bawarchis! I forgot.'

'Luckily for you, I didn't,' Suraiya said smugly, flying to the pantry on a rescue mission.

Divumber stuck his tongue out at her. Then, he dashed back to Awadh Mahal to release Gajodhar.

***

'I'm so sorry,' Suraiya said earnestly, as Roshanara staggered out of the pantry. 'There's a very good explanation...'

The young woman grimaced, hopping on one foot. 'It'll have to wait. Really need to...'

Suraiya's expression cleared. '...use the washroom? Of course!'

***

After everyone apologised profusely to Roshanara and Gajodhar and the dazed chefs went back home, the grandchildren and grandparents got ready to leave.

'You two!' admonished Mataji. 'And here I thought the other drama was the highlight of the evening.'

'What other drama?' asked the tweens.

'The Machli Committee was forced to reveal the identity of a Machli Star Inspector...she went missing for *hours*,'

DJ explained. 'They launched a massive manhunt-uh, womanhunt? The search party finally found her stumbling around in the bhool bhulaiya...'

Suraiya and Divumber gasped.

'Inspector Chulbul? *She* is the Machli Star Inspector?'

'They hide in plain sight,' chuckled Mataji.

'Told you,' chortled DJ.

Suraiya and Divumber exchanged a glance. So that's why Chulbul was hanging around their restaurants all the time!

'She said she's been meaning to quit for months,' DJ clucked.

'After tonight's adventure, she certainly will,' Mataji remarked.

'Minus the Pasinabad Pulao recipe!' Suraiya-Divumber chorused triumphantly.

Mataji sighed. '*You* sent Inspector Chulbul on a wild goose chase, didn't you?'

Suraiya and Divumber grinned.

'Why am I not surprised?' DJ muttered, shaking his head.

***

A few days later, Ammi walked into Shaan-e-Daawat, looking crumpled (or maybe that was just her clothes since she'd travelled halfway around the world), worried and dazed.

'Ammi!' Suraiya whooped, running into her arms, hugging her tight.

'Su?' began Ammi, when they broke away. 'What're you doing here? At this time of the night? You said you were down with high fever, rashes, infection and whatnot the last time we spoke.'

Suraiya's face flushed.

'I got on the next available flight... rushed home but a Khala...or was that a Phuppee...never mind, not important. She said Abbu and you'd be here. I don't understand. Where's Abbu? What's going on?'

'I think I know,' came a familiar voice. Familiar to Ammi, that is.

Ammi whirled around to find Divumber and his Papa standing at the entrance. 'Swayam,' she gasped. 'What are you doing here?'

'Same thing you are, Ghazal.' Divumber's Papa looked crushed, (or maybe that was just his shirt after travelling thousands of miles) and tired. He looked at Divumber. 'He told me he was down with high fever, rashes, infection and whatnot.'

Divumber's face flamed.

That's what it had taken to bring Ammi and Papa rushing back to Pasinabad.

'We did the wrong thing for the right reason, Ammi.'

Papa loosened his tie and settled down on a table. So did Ammi. Except, she didn't loosen her tie (she wasn't wearing one).

'Sorry, Ammi,' said Suraiya.

'Sorry, Papa,' said Divumber, when they finished narrating the story.

'Wow!' said Ammi.

'Your DJ and your Mataji went to a lot of trouble to bring you together,' said Papa.

They looked at each other without speaking for a whole minute. (It felt longer.) Then, they nodded quietly.

'I'm so glad the families are on talking terms again,' said Ammi, 'but...'

'...if you both went to all this trouble to bring *us* together,' said Papa, 'I'm afraid...'

'I've already given my heart away to someone,' admitted Ammi.

Suraiya screeched like a skidding tyre. 'I knew it! I knew it the minute you said let's move to California.'

'There's someone special in my life, too,' confessed Papa.

'Noooo!' Divumber burst out like a leaky pipe.

There was a moment of pained silence, then Ammi and Papa burst out laughing.

Suraiya and Divumber stared at them, dumbfounded.

'And that's how you prank someone!'

'We still make a great team!'

Ammi and Papa high-fived, low-fived.

Suraiya and Divumber gasped, then shrieked with delight, then rushed forward to group hug.

'Speaking of teamwork, there's something we need to do,' Suraiya informed Papa and Ammi strictly.

'Win Machli Stars for the restaurants,' Divumber said.

'So, here's what you two are going to make.'

Ammi and Papa raised their eyebrows. '*We*?'

Suraiya and Divumber beamed. 'Nimona Lajawaab!'

PETU TIMES

The Pride of Pasinabad! Shaan-e-Daawat and Awadh Mahal, winners of the prestigious Machli Stars!'

Acknowledgements

ROYAL DECREE

By order of His Majesty Nawab Naak-Mein-Dum

For crafting the legendary Peace Pulao with passion, precision and perfection, it is hereby decreed that

Foodie Family; Rakabdar Tina Narang; Daroga-e-bawarchikhana Aparna Kapur;

Food Inspector Nimmy Chacko; Food Stylist Sucharita Sengupta; Dastarkhawan HarperCollins; Masala Box Friends; Food Taster Readers; Food Critic HP

are officially declared to be members of the Pasinabad Court. Furthermore, they are accorded bronze plaques and honorary titles, and shall forthwith be known as Naak-Mein-Dum's Navratnas.

May the feasting and merrymaking commence.

Royal Seal

His Royal Highness Nawab Naak-Mein-Dum

Vibha Batra is an author, graphic novelist, advertising consultant, poet, lyricist, translator, playwright, script writer, travel writer, columnist, speaker and creative writing mentor. She has published 30 books across genres and over 100 short stories. Her books have won prestigious awards, bestseller tags and readers' hearts.

HarperCollins *Publishers* India

At HarperCollins India, we believe in telling the best stories and finding the widest readership for our books in every format possible. We started publishing in 1992; a great deal has changed since then, but what has remained constant is the passion with which our authors write their books, the love with which readers receive them, and the sheer joy and excitement that we as publishers feel in being a part of the publishing process.

Over the years, we've had the pleasure of publishing some of the finest writing from the subcontinent and around the world, including several award-winning titles and some of the biggest bestsellers in India's publishing history. But nothing has meant more to us than the fact that millions of people have read the books we published, and that somewhere, a book of ours might have made a difference.

As we look to the future, we go back to that one word—a word which has been a driving force for us all these years.

Read.

Harper Collins · 4th · HARPER FICTION · HARPER NON-FICTION · HARPER BUSINESS · HC CB

HARPER DESIGN · Harper Sport · HARPER PERENNIAL · HARPER VANTAGE · हार्पर हिन्दी · BOOKTOPUS

Menaka Raman is an author, dog petter and plant killer. She has written picture books, chapter books and middle grade novels. She has been known to hide the Nutella jar and eat straight from it after everyone else has gone to sleep.

The Forbidden Snacks Society

The Forbidden Snacks Society

MENAKA RAMAN

HarperCollins*Children'sBooks*

First published in India by HarperCollins *Children's* Books 2025
An imprint of HarperCollins *Publishers*
HarperCollins *Publishers* India, Cyber City,
Building 10-A, Gurugram, Haryana-122002, India
www.harpercollins.co.in

2 4 6 8 10 9 7 5 3 1

P-ISBN: 978-93-6989-240-2
E-ISBN: 978-93-6989-817-6

Typeset in 12/16.3 Scala Sans Pro
by HarperCollins *Publishers* India Pvt. Ltd

Printed and bound at
Thomson Press (India) Ltd

MIX
Paper | Supporting responsible forestry
FSC® C010615

This book is produced from independently certified FSC® paper to ensure responsible forest management.

HarperCollins Publishers, Macken House, 39/40 Mayor Street Upper,
Dublin 1, D01 C9W8, Ireland

This book is for everyone who has ever lovingly made me a snack or shared one with me. Thank you.

Contents

1

Just Grit and Bear It

ANIKA SLUMPED DOWN AND PULLED the hood of her sweatshirt over her face and scowled. She felt the toddler-like urge to kick the car seat in front of her, but remembered that she was thirteen years old and not three. Also, it would serve no purpose other than to lead to a long lecture about opportunities, gratitude, success, privilege and a list of other things her father wrote about in his weekly productivity newsletter, *Grit and Bear It*.

She sensed her parents exchanging a look with each other and rolled her eyes.

'Ani,' her mother said, adopting a low and soothing voice she often used with her clients.

'What?'

'Are you rolling your eyes at us?'

God. How did her mother know these things? She said that it was a mother's job to know stuff like that about their children—what they were feeling, thinking and doing—and till this summer, Ani had believed that. But now she wasn't

so sure. If her mother *really* knew how she felt, she wouldn't be sending Ani away like this.

'Why do you care?'

Her mother let out a long sigh.

'Ani, how many times do we have to tell you this is not a punishment? It's an opportunity,' her father started. 'A chance to see what you're really made of. Do you know how many young people would give anything to exchange places with you right now?'

Ani felt a cloud of anger gather around her. She leaned forward in her seat as much as her seat belt would allow and pulled her hoodie back.

'Really? There are young people out there who would give anything to be shunted off to fat camp for three whole weeks while their parents go to Europe together on "work"? Sure! I can see them just lining up!'

'It's not a fat camp, and you know I don't like you using that word,' her mother said.

'Oh, I'm so sorry! How could I forget? It's a "wellness space" for people who happen to be short and dumpy like me! I'm done with this conversation—wake me up when we get there.'

Ani fell back into her seat, pulled her noise-cancelling headphones on and turned the music on her phone all the way up. As Bikini Kill's *Rebel Girl* started up she stared out of the window at the passing highway. Every now and then a roadside food stall selling vada pav would appear. Her mouth filled with saliva at the thought of sinking her teeth into a soft pav, the insides slathered with spicy garlic chutney. She almost swallowed her pride and asked her father to pull

over, but held back, not wanting one of her parents to say, ‘But we just ate lunch! How are you hungry again?’ which was parent-speak for ‘this is why you’re going to a fat camp while we attend an international mental health conference in Croatia’. She wondered if the irony of it all was lost on them.

Not that the place they were sending her to was actually called a ‘fat camp’. Oh no, she was being sent to the Temple of Mind and Body Excellence, a wellness and detox retreat run by a former collegemate of her mother’s, who wanted to help young people kick whatever it was they were addicted to: their phones, gaming, social media and, in Ani’s case, doughnuts covered in chocolate glazing. And cheese dosa. And butter biscuits. And pretty much anything that was not kale, quinoa or karela.

Ani was convinced that if she had been born to normal parents, her love for good food would not have been an issue. But her parents were tall, athletic ultramarathoners who had green juice flowing through their veins and whose idea of fun was weight training and push-up challenges. They counted macros and micros and protein in grams and were up at four every morning to get ‘a head start to the day’. They hosted a podcast called *Two Peas in Health Pod*—gross—and were always being interviewed by a YouTube channel or digital magazine about their fitness goals. It was disgusting.

Ani, on the other hand, was short, liked to trek because, duh, mountains were beautiful, and strongly believed that if the universe didn’t want her to eat pistachio-flavoured macarons, it wouldn’t have given someone the idea to create them. And yes, she was plump. Or as one of her more horrible

classmates had yelled as they'd driven by her at the bus stop one morning last year, a 'whale'. Unfortunately, for Ani and her classmate, her mother had been on her morning run at the same time and overheard this, which led to a demand for an apology, sensitivity training about body image for all seventh graders at school and an exhausting hyperfocus on what Ani ate and how much she exercised.

'Shall we do sugar-free September?' 'Do you really want to eat a biscuit right now?' 'Shall we sign up for Mommy and Me Krav Maga?'

When her parents suggested she spend half her summer vacation at camp, Ani had assumed it would be the kind of adventure camp she usually went to. But then they'd shown her the brochure for this place which said 'This is your chance to cleanse, heal and reset your child in the pristine Sahyadri Hills'. When she'd asked where *her* reset button was, they hadn't joined in her laughter.

'Why do I need to go here? I don't need resetting. I'm not some robot, Ma,' she'd said.

'We think you'd benefit from a little more discipline and rigour in your life, Ani. Learn to make better choices!' her mother had offered in response.

Her? Make better choices? She made the *best* choices. Who wouldn't rather stay in bed and cuddle their dog and read a book instead of going for a run on a Sunday morning? In the rain!

'Correct! I like to put tasty things in my mouth and treat my body to rest and relaxation. What's wrong with that?' she'd demanded. 'So what if I don't want to get up at 4 a.m. and run around a track like a lunatic?'

What had followed was A) a massive fight, B) a ceasefire during which Ani had assumed she wasn't being sent away but was going to Croatia, C) the realization that she was indeed still going to fat camp, which led to another massive fight, D) an attempt to run away to her grandmother's house, E) a humiliating return home and then waking up one morning to find a packed rucksack at the foot of her bed.

And so here she was, on her way to three weeks of learning mind and body excellence. If her stomach hadn't been empty, Ani was sure she'd have thrown up by now.

2

The Absolutely Perfect Bubble Boy

ABHANINDRANATH SENGUPTA SWATTED AT THE giant mosquito buzzing around him.

'Sit still, Bubbles!' his father hissed.

Two girls seated in the row ahead of theirs heard his father and turned around. Abhanindranath aka Bubbles was delighted to discover that they were twins. He'd never met twins before! But they responded to his smile with an eye roll and a smirk that he wasn't sure was entirely friendly.

'Baba, I told you not to call me that!' Abhanindranath/ Bubbles whispered back.

'But why?' His father looked confused. 'That's your name.'

'My name is Abhanindranath! A-bha-nin-dra-nath. It says so on my passport. Why don't you ever call me that?'

Not that Abhanindranath was any better than Bubbles, he thought sourly. It sounded like the name of a dead nineteenth-century artist. Which is exactly what it was.

'What's gotten into you? You used to love being called Bubbles. Remember how you used to sing "I'm a Bubble Boy"—'

'Baba! Shhhh!' Bubbles cut in, shooting a look at the twins who were now laughing openly. Great. Bubbles didn't think his summer vacation could have gotten off to a worse start. First, his parents had rejected his idea of attending culinary camp like he'd wanted to, then they'd refused to send him to the camp he usually attended with his friends, and finally, as if that wasn't bad enough, they had decided to send him to a place with an utterly strange and, frankly, scary-sounding name: TOMBE. And now, instead of allowing him to brand himself as a cool and mysterious rising chef, everyone would know he was called Bubbles and that he used to sing 'I'm a Bubble Boy' when he was younger. Okay, maybe he still sang it when he was making himself a snack, but no one needed to know that.

The amphitheatre was filled with children and their parents, and there was an expectant buzz in the air, sprinkled with a dash of nervousness. Bubbles had to admit, TOMBE was a beautiful, if mosquito-ridden, place. The amphitheatre was surrounded by trees, which were decorated with twinkling fairy lights. Hidden from view were the cabins where the campers would stay and the cafeteria where all the meals were served. Bubbles was looking forward to seeing what the breakfast buffet offered.

He leaned forward a bit and tapped one of the girls on her shoulder.

'Hi! I'm Abhi!' he said, trying out the new nickname he'd recently given himself. 'I'm a YouTuber. You might have seen

my channel? Breakfast with Bubb—umm, Abhi? It has 2500 followers and I make interesting breakfast items from around the world!'

'Oh my god! I thought I recognized you!' one of the girls gushed.

Bubbles smiled, not even bothering to hide the massive gap between his front teeth. 'Really?' he asked.

'Uh, no! Of course not. Who wants to watch a YouTube channel dedicated to poha and idli?' the other girl replied.

'Oh! But I have a perfect poha recipe on my channel! It's delicious. You should try it! The secret ingredient is—'

'Bubbles, remember why you're here,' his father interrupted, 'to overcome your YouTube obsession. To try new things that are not screen and food-related. To broaden your horizons. YouTubing is not a real thing.'

Bubbles wanted to tell his father that YouTubing was not a word and that the 65.3 million YouTubers around the world would disagree that what they did wasn't real. And that he loved cooking. And that he *was* broadening his horizons. The summer workshop he'd wanted to attend was on fermentation, something he'd been interested in for months. But Baba was convinced that *Breakfast with Bubbles* (recently renamed *Breakfast with Abhi*) was a distraction from 'more worthy pursuits that he should be striving for'.

So here he was at the Temple of Mind and Body Excellence, a place that Baba promised would exorcise him and the other children of their addictions and bad habits. Bubbles had looked up 'exorcism' on YouTube and had not slept for a week.

Bubbles didn't see why he needed to be exorcised or detoxed or whatever. He was absolutely perfect as he was. His Dida told him this all the time, and she was the smartest woman he knew.

'Baba, look, I think—'

Bubbles was cut short as the amphitheatre suddenly plunged into darkness. Some of the audience screamed a little in surprise and panicked chatter broke out, but it quietened a bit when a single, powerful spotlight fell on the stage, revealing a large, padlocked trunk. *Where had that come from?*

A voice blared across the speakers.

'Are your children being limited by their laziness? Are they sidetracked by social media? What is the link between the Ds on their report card and the doughnuts they're mindlessly shoving into their mouths? How can they channel their energy into endeavours that serve society and not just themselves? How can they harness the limitless power of their minds and bodies for excellence? What can we do to ensure they treat their bodies like temples and not toilets?'

The trunk on the stage was now vibrating and everyone was staring at it intently. Every time it moved a little, the audience jumped a little too.

'Over the next three weeks we will transform your progeny! Your children will no longer be your children but vessels of our great nation's glory and pride, thanks to our soon-to-be-patented novel approach of sweat, seva and salt-free food.'

A multitude of strobe lights began to flash across the stage while thumping music began to play.

‘Ladies and gentlemen, boys and girls, welcome to the Temple of Mind and Body Excellence! Please put your hands together and welcome biohacker extraordinaire, genius scientist, black belt in jiu-jitsu, the man who is reversing his age and will one day trick death, our sensei, our guru, our leader, our reason for existing, and YOUR SAVIOUR! Dr. K.K.K. Kiran!’

A rain of confetti fell across the stage as the trunk burst open.

3

Misshapen Lumps of Clay

VASU LOOKED AROUND THE CABIN he was expected to inhabit for the next three weeks of his sweat, seva and salt-free life. The room was much smaller than his bedroom back home, but whoever had designed it had managed to fit in a bunk bed, a writing desk and chair and two small cupboards. There was a lone poster on the wall which proclaimed: 'What seems impossible today will one day be your warm-up.' He didn't like the sound of that.

Vasu didn't like *anything* about TOMBE. The induction event had been all headache-inducing lights, confetti showers and flame throwers (a combination his father muttered was 'a terrible fire hazard'). When the padlocked trunk on stage had burst open, it revealed a surprisingly small man wearing a very tight muscle tee that showed off some very large muscles. He looked like the superhero figurines that Vasu used to play with when he was in primary school. Even his skin had a certain stretched, plasticky quality to it, something that the jumbotron screens on the stage revealed. Dr. K.K.K. Kiran, the guru-scientist-saviour-jiu-jitsu-black belt, was then

hoisted onto the shoulders of a group of men and women wearing t-shirts emblazoned with I <3 MY TOMBE.

After the confetti had settled on the stage, the man had taken his shirt off and then dropped to his hands and feet to do a series of push-ups—knuckle push-ups, normal push-ups, one-handed push-ups, diamond-shaped push-ups and archer push-ups. He had even invited someone from the audience to come and sit on his back while he did the push-ups, and for a terrifying moment, Vasu's mother had looked like she was going to volunteer. Thankfully she didn't.

'Do you want to win? Be a winner? Succeed? Be successful? Advance? Be advanced? All you need is control: over your minds, your bodies, your bowel movements, your caloric intake,' Dr. K.K.K. Kiran had said into what Vasu had to admit was a pretty cool-looking headset.

'The problem is that you have NO control! You've handed it over to smartphones, social media, algorithms, junk food, and binge-watching cat videos!' he thundered as he became a blur on the stage, now skipping rope at a dizzying speed. His team stood on the sidelines, armed with towels, water bottles and what appeared to be an unending stream of encouraging whoops, claps and cheers.

'How many of you know that your children are out of control? How many of you have told me this? ALL OF YOU! That is why you have given me control of your spawn so that they are no longer parasites feeding off society. I will take these misshapen lumps of clay and mould them to perfection and return them to you: sharp of mind, sharp of body, sharp of soul! Members of our great nation's future army, helping it forge ahead to greater glory!'

Vasu had turned to his parents convinced that this nonsensical and alarming speech was what it would take for them to get up, head to the parking lot with him and then drive back to Pune and catch the next flight to Delhi. But they seemed to be in some kind of bizarre trance: their eyes were wide open and they were swaying to the beat of the hypnotic music playing.

'Mom, Dad! You can't seriously be thinking of leaving me here? He just called me a parasite! Please let's go home. You can take all my devices, melt them and make tiny cubes with them if you want, just don't leave me here!'

'Don't worry, son. You'll thank us for this one day! It's going to be a transformative experience,' his father had replied.

On stage, Dr. K.K.K. Kiran continued. 'The Temple of Mind and Body Excellence is the answer to our society's malaise! We must be fit in body and thought, we must purge ourselves of the toxic poison that has invaded our souls, we must return to our roots! We are hunter-gatherers! We shall not be slaves to carbs and couches! Rise and let the world hear you roar, young ones!'

Vasu's mother had taken his hand and squeezed it lovingly. 'Roar, darling! Go on!'

He looked at her in disbelief. His mother saw the look on his face and smiled encouragingly, sipping her second green 'welcome' drink of the evening.

'Look! Look at these children! They're right here. They aren't voices in your ear while you play those awful video games about eating brains. Once you spend time with them and get to know them, they'll be your best friends. Real best friends,' she said.

And there it was, the reason he was here. His parents would never understand what his online friends meant to him. Real kids—the ones his mother seemed to think were so great—were routinely horrible to him; at least the ones at his school were. They made fun of everything about him: his height—he was too tall, his weight—there was too much of it, and his hair—no matter how he cut it, it was never right.

When he'd complained that he was being bullied, his classmates had told the teacher that they were just roasting him, a sign of social acceptance. Then they'd taken him to the boys' bathroom and held him down over a toilet and said he needed to get a sense of humour. So he'd joined in and made fun of himself along with them the next day, but they'd asked him why he didn't have any self-respect. There was just no winning.

But when he was gaming, all his fellow players could see was his online avatar, Archer Babylon: a super muscular mercenary who could do double flips in the air, slay zombies and had a crossbow made of titanium called Vlad the Impaler.

So the meaner the kids were to him at school—and they all seemed to have gotten meaner this past year—the more he turned to his online friends, and the more his parents lectured him about going outside and playing with real children in the fresh air. Which was funny considering how Gurgaon's AQI had broken all previous records that year.

When an announcement on the PA system had instructed the parents to bid goodbye to their wards and leave in an orderly fashion, Vasu had grabbed their hands and begged them to take him home. But they had just smiled, patted

his head, and promised that everything would be okay. Then they'd dumped him at the door of his cabin and left.

Vasu's cabinmate was missing, though they had left their suitcase on one of the beds. The name tag on it read 'Bubbles Sengupta', which was, objectively speaking, a terrible name.

Vasu threw his rucksack in a corner and lay down on the bed. It was 7 p.m.— his team would all be online, playing and talking and making battle plans. And here he was, alone in the middle of nowhere.

4

A Laddoo Tug-of-War

NAVJYOT HAD TO ADMIT, THE cabin looked like a luxury hotel compared to the hostels she usually stayed in when training or competing. There was a lingering smell of paint, the bed didn't have icky-looking stains on it and the windows had brightly checked white-and-blue curtains that fluttered in the evening breeze.

'Wow! Can I stay here too?' Navjyot's younger sister Chikki piped up. 'I also want a holiday!'

'Shush. Enough from you!' their father said, but a smile curved his lips.

Navjyot snorted. Of course, with Chikki her father was all sweet smiles and hush-shush and sunshine. But when it came to her, Navjyot's father's inner drill sergeant took over, and it was all barks, grunts, one-word commands and a permanently furrowed brow. Their relationship was about 4 a.m. wake-up calls, running, training, eating right and then the same thing over and over again.

Navjyot was a good wrestler. But she wasn't the best. Not yet anyway. And according to her new coach, all that

stood between her and state-level greatness was discipline and curbing her innate need to poke her nose in things that didn't concern her. 'She talks back and has her own ideas about everything: why do the boys get more training time, why can't I train with them, why do they get more milk to drink? Sir! Champions are made by doing as they are told not telling the coach what they want to do. Plus, she needs to lose a couple of kilograms to stay in her current category.'

Then Coach had heard of a new camp in the Sahyadris that promised a fit body and disciplined mind, and he had sent her parents the brochure insisting they sign her up for it. And they had. Worse, they'd spent a small fortune on it. A small fortune their family didn't really have. Which meant that Navjyot had no choice but to pack a bag and get on the train.

'Yeah, Chikki, this is going to be a real holiday for me. Dr. Kiran seems like a load of laughs!' Navjyot said sarcastically.

'Show some respect for your elders!' her father snapped.

Navjyot's mother, adept at picking up the signs of a fight brewing between father and daughter, intervened. 'Have a sattu laddoo, Navjyot. I've made enough to last a month so you can share them with your friends. Remember to keep this in a shallow basin of water so the ants don't get to it,' she said, opening a steel dabba and pushing it towards her.

Just then, the door to the cabin opened and a young woman wearing an I <3 MY TOMBE T-shirt stepped inside, followed by a very short girl wearing a hoodie three sizes too big for her and a mean scowl.

'Here's your room, Anika. You'll be sharing with Jyothi,' the counsellor said in a voice devoid of all emotion.

'*Navjyot*. Not Jyothi. My name is Navjyot!' she said through gritted teeth.

The girl called Anika looked Navjyot up and down with wide eyes. 'You're massive!'

Navjyot was now even more annoyed. Yes, she was tall and strong, but she didn't like the way people felt it was completely okay to make observations about her appearance like that.

'Well, of course I'd appear massive to you. You stopped growing in kindergarten!'

'Navjyot, that's not very nice,' her mother admonished before proffering the dabba to Anika. 'Here, beta, take a laddoo. You also take one,' she added, nodding to the counsellor.

The other woman's eyes narrowed as she took in the dabba. 'No outside food is allowed on the premises! This will be confiscated and destroyed!'

Navjyot's mother laughed at the absurdity of anyone destroying her laddoos. 'Don't be silly! I just made them yesterday.'

'Inmates can only eat food prepared on campus under the strict supervision of Dr. Basith and Dr. Kiran,' the counsellor replied firmly, reaching for the dabba.

Inmates? Navjyot thought. *It makes the place sound like a prison.*

'Please hand the dabba over, Madam.'

'But this is healthy! It's made with sattu and jaggery. No sugar, no oil, no ghee,' her mother replied, pulling the dabba towards her chest.

Navjyot heard Anika mutter 'No taste' under her breath.

Who was *she* to say her mother's laddoos were tasteless? 'Hey! They're made from my great-great-grandmother's laddoo recipe and they're great, okay?' Navjyot growled at her.

'Madam, please hand it over,' the counsellor said, grabbing hold of the dabba.

Navjyot's mother pulled it back and soon the two women were playing a kind of tug-of-war with it.

'Madam, we must destroy any and all contraband before there is contamination within TOMBE,' the woman grunted as she tugged hard.

Navjyot's mother was a tall and well-built woman, physical traits that she had inherited from her family of tall and well-built people. In comparison, the counsellor was a wiry little thing who couldn't have weighed more than 43 kg. And yet, her grip on the steel dabba was strong and she didn't seem intimidated by the other woman's size. Anika had sat down on a bed to watch the unfolding events with interest.

'Do you want some popcorn?' Navjyot snapped.

'I'd say yes, but that probably comes under their list of contraband items,' Anika replied with a smirk.

Navjyot's father finally intervened.

'Let go of the dabba, Simran,' he told her mother. 'We brought her here to learn some discipline. How will she do that if we go about breaking rules ourselves? Come on. Hand it over. We need to go anyway. I don't want to be driving back to the station late at night. There might be wild animals crossing.'

'Wild animals?' Anika asked. 'What wild animals? No one said anything about wild animals to me!'

'Do not worry. Any threats to TOMBE from Sector 2 and surrounding areas will be neutralized with immediate effect,' the line dripped off the counsellor's tongue in a smooth, well-rehearsed way.

'N-n-no. I don't want you to neutralize anything!' Anika said.

'Nice going, shorty!' sneered Navjyot.

'Don't call me shorty, I have at least another three growth spurts to go, okay?'

'Got any weight loss spurts to go too? You could afford to lose a few kgs!'

Navjyot regretted the words the minute they left her mouth. She knew what it was like to have people say mean things about one's size. She was a *big* girl, and for years she'd been taunted by her classmates, neighbours and even relatives. A hurt look crossed Anika's face, and Navjyot wanted to apologize but somehow couldn't bring herself to.

'I want another cabin. I cannot share a room with her!' Anika said to the counsellor.

'All cabins are occupied. No room change requests will be entertained at this time,' the counsellor said.

'I'm going to tell my father about this.' Anika took her phone out and began to swipe and tap when the counsellor snatched it out of her hand.

'Hey! Give me that! It's mine!' Anika yelled.

'Phones, computers, laptops, tablets and facsimile machines are not allowed inside TOMBE.'

Anika looked blank. 'What's a facsimile machine?'

'It is a machine used for sending faxes,' the counsellor replied.

'What's a fax?' asked Chikki.

'A fax is short for facsimile. It's a—'

'Oh never mind. I don't care! I just want my phone back,' said Anika, actually stomping her foot.

'Sorry, that will not be possible. Now, it is time for I, Saritha, to retire for the evening to rest and recharge. Parents, I request you to take leave of your ward and leave the premises. Inmates must be in bed by 8.30 p.m. for the 4 a.m. wake-up call.'

'4 a.m. wake-up call?' Anika wailed. 'No one told me anything about that either!'

Oh this is going to be fun, thought Navjyot.

5

The Floor Is Lava. (Not Really.)

BUBBLES COULD NOT REMEMBER THE last time he'd been awake at 4 a.m. It was still dark outside, and the air was deliciously cool and crisp, like the first bite of a Kinnaur apple. When a shrill and winding siren had rung out over the PA system, Bubbles had thought the camp was on fire. He'd fallen out of his bed, scrambled to the door and flung it open, ready to run to safety. Only to be stopped by a thick, hairy arm on his shoulder. It was attached to a very large, muscled camp counsellor.

'Where do you think you're going dressed like that? Change into one of the track suits provided in your cupboard, then come to the activity field,' the counsellor had barked.

Disoriented, Bubbles had done as he was told, and joined the trickle of boys and girls making their way towards what he assumed was the activity field.

When Bubbles saw that everyone was standing in pairs, a wave of dismay washed over him. Where was his cabinmate? Was he still asleep in the cabin? Should he go back and wake him up? Did he even *have* a cabinmate? The questions

buzzing in his head fell silent when he sensed that he was being watched. And he was. A woman wearing a blinding white lab coat was standing in front of the group of campers with five counsellors on either side of her.

The woman said nothing, but her eyes bored into Bubbles's soul, which was silly, because they were eyes, not drills, and also Bubbles didn't know if souls were real and if they were, where was his? Was it in his big toe or left earlobe? The woman's eyes moved from child to child till their nervous chatter subsided.

'Good morning, TOMBE inmates! Welcome to the start of your journey towards a new and improved you! I am Dr. Basith, Dr. Kiran's partner and C.O.W.—Chief of Wellness—here at TOMBE. Dr. Kiran wanted to be here for your first morning at TOMBE but this activity clashed with his daily DNA methylation test. But there will be plenty of opportunities for you all to meet and interact with your saviour. My role here is to ensure that over the next three weeks you shed your former slothful selves and learn to take control of your dead minds and flabby bodies. Each and every day you will arise and push yourselves to the very limits of your physical and mental abilities. But before we wade into this arduous journey of renewal, we thought it would be fun to start with a game!'

Oooh! Bubbles thought. He loved games.

'This morning, we will play "The Floor is Lava"! TOMBE Style!' the woman announced enthusiastically.

The campers broke out into excited chatter. A girl next to Bubbles turned to an extraordinarily tall girl and asked, 'Didn't you play this when you were a kid? The floor is molten

lava and you have to get from one side to the other without touching the floor!'

The tall girl looked confused. 'How? By flying?'

The short girl rolled her eyes. 'No, dodo—which is an extinct, flightless bird by the way—you can use anything other than the floor: furniture, cushions, whatever you find.'

'Which mother lets her kids climb on the furniture? Not mine!'

Bubbles chimed in with a 'Same here!' and the girls looked back at him.

'Eavesdropping, much?' the shorter girl asked.

'You're so loud they can hear you over in the next state,' the tall one sniped and then turned to Bubbles. 'Hi! I'm Navjyot and this is Anika. What's your name?'

'Bub-Abhi.'

'Bubabhi? What kind of name is that?' asked Anika.

'Abhi, my name is Abhi,' he said. The girl shrugged and turned back to Dr. Basith.

'The mud field has been laid out with items which you can use to cross over. If any part of your body touches the mud field you're out! The team with the maximum number of participants to get across first wins a special prize.'

Dr. Basith paused and looked around once before dramatically announcing, 'BREAKFAST!'

Bubbles felt some of his pleasure at the idea of playing a game deflate.

'What about the teams that lose? They don't get breakfast?' asked a voice from the back.

'Oh, don't worry, we won't be starving any of you, though some of you could benefit from intermittent

fasting. The winning team gets a very special, one-of-a-kind breakfast! So, you better get going. Divide yourselves into teams of five. Come on!'

Bubbles looked at the two girls. 'Can I join your team? I don't know where my cabinmate is.'

'Sure!'

Navjyot scanned the crowd and then headed off to find two other teammates. She returned soon with the twins Bubbles had tried to talk to the previous evening in the amphitheatre.

'Abhi, Anika, meet Mansi and Meera,' Navjyot said.

'I thought your name was Bubbles,' one of them said, pointing at him.

'That's my daak naam—my pet name. Abhi is short for Abhanindranath, my bhalo naam—good name. You can call me whatever you like,' he offered.

The twins made an identical expression of displeasure before one of them turned to Anika and said, 'Not him. Let's find someone else.'

Bubbles shrank back a little and turned to leave when he heard Anika ask, 'Why should he leave? He was here first. If you want to, you leave.'

Bubbles shot her a grateful look and watched the twins look around. Everyone else had formed teams already so they shrugged and agreed to stay but not before one of them, Mansi...or maybe it was Meera, pointed a finger at Bubbles and said, 'Do not mess this up for us. We want to win that special breakfast, okay?'

Navjyot snorted and hustled them all to one of the ten starting points that dotted the boundary line of the activity field.

'Let's study what they've laid out on the course. Everyone else will just charge and try to get across but we have to be strategic,' she told the others.

'Who made you the boss of us?' asked one of the twins. Navjyot turned around, straightened her back and looked down at all of them from her very immense height.

'I'm not anyone's boss or captain. I'm just stating facts. We need a plan. Do you have one?'

Mansi sniffed. 'I can't think properly till I've had a caramel macchiato to wake up my brain cells.'

Anika sniggered and whispered loudly, 'What brain cells?'

Navjyot ignored them and turned back to the field, studying the items laid out. Each group had a small pile of bricks, a longish wooden plank, a large plastic basin, what looked like a folded blanket, a gunny sack and a ladder.

Bubbles felt a wave of panic wash over him. How were they meant to get across to the other side of the activity field with such few items?

'Right, here's what we're going to do!' Navjyot said, beckoning them to gather around her and shared her plan.

Navjyot was first in their line-up, followed by Anika, the twins and finally Bubbles, who felt nervous about being last. What if they forgot he was there?

One of the counsellors blew a whistle and yelled, 'Inmates! On your marks, get set and gooooo!'

The first item in the line-up was a set of four bricks arranged vertically. Bubbles watched as Navjyot nimbly leapt to the first one and then leaned forward, tossing the remaining bricks, one by one, so that they formed a pathway

of sorts for her and the rest of the team. As she bounded forward, she yelled over her back, 'Anika, start!'

Bubbles watched as they each moved forward. Anika was not as confident as Navjyot, but still managed to land on each brick, as did the twins. Bubbles caught sight of the other teams. Some of them had followed Navjyot's lead and used the bricks for a pathway, but the ones who hadn't stood unsure of what to do on their island of bricks, getting yelled at by their teammates to find a way forward. In one group, a teammate surged forward and pushed the first camper off the bricks to take the spot and move ahead.

When it was Bubbles's turn, he took a deep breath and stretched his leg as far as he could. He was still about an inch short of the brick.

'Abhi!' Anika yelled from ahead. She was walking on the long wooden plank with the twins behind her. 'You need a big leap forward for the first brick. The others aren't too far apart, it's just the first one that's a stretch.'

Bubbles nodded back at her but then felt like his brain had ceased communicating with his body. *What was a leap again?*

'Hurry up!' Anika shouted. Bubbles saw the look of disgust on the twins' faces, which made him feel even worse.

All around him teams were advancing. The campers who had fallen down, or placed a hand or foot on the mud field were immediately identified by the counsellors who blew their whistles and yelled the numbers emblazoned on the backs of their jackets, before pulling them to the sidelines.

Bubbles took a deep breath and jumped—or leapt—and landed on the brick. He made it to the last brick quickly and then hopped on to the wooden plank, which he realized was not as broad as he thought it would be, and raised on stilts that made it sway with every step he took.

Ahead, Navjyot was standing in the large shallow plastic basin and shuffling forward. The minute she reached the next item—a blanket—she jumped on to it and then bent forward and tossed the basin through the air to Anika who caught it.

By the time Bubbles reached the end of the wooden plank, one of the twins—Mansi...or was it Meera?—had finished using the basin and swept her arms way behind her before throwing it. Except, it didn't reach Bubbles at all; it sailed right over his head and landed somewhere behind him.

'Oops!' the girl giggled, 'I guess I'm not very good at throwing things.'

6

Evil Twins and the Necromancer of Nagasandra

'HEY! I SAW THAT. You did it on purpose!' Anika said, looking over at Bubbles who was standing at the end of the plank looking unsure and terrified.

'Of course I did! He's a deadweight. He'll just hold us back. If the four of us make it across we can still win that breakfast! And there'll be more for us to eat!' Mansi said, shoving at Anika, who didn't budge.

'My mother doesn't call me her little tank for nothing. You'll have to push me a lot harder than that,' Anika sneered and then turned to Navjyot. 'We have to help Bubbles. We can't just leave him there!'

Navjyot was holding the blanket in her hands and staring at it, as though wondering how to use it.

'Bubbles! Take your jacket off and put it on the ground and then shuffle across on it! Come on, we don't have much time left,' she said, pointing to a counsellor standing near

the finish line with a massive clock in his hands, its red digits blinking as they descended towards zero.

'Listen to her,' Anika yelled when she saw Bubbles hesitate. 'And hurry!'

Bubbles unzipped his jacket slowly, swaying precariously as he peeled it off, before dropping it on the ground. He then jumped down, and waddled forward as best as he could with his two feet firmly planted on top of his jacket.

Up and down the field, campers had turned into screaming, raging banshees. Some were in tears as they picked themselves up off the ground, others sullen and disqualified on the sidelines, watching the remaining campers move ahead with barely disguised hatred. This was nothing like the games Bubbles played with his friends. He felt a frisson of fear down his spine, as he saw one camper throw their plastic basin at another team's basin and knock it out of their pathway.

When Bubbles reached the others, he struggled back into his dusty jacket as Navjyot wrapped one of the twins up in the blanket like a kathi roll. Anika crouched over her and hissed, 'Double-cross one of us again and see where that gets you!' before they both gave her a shove. They watched her roll across to the gunny bag and struggle into an upright position with her feet on the sack. She then folded the blanket deftly and tied the ends together so it was like a parcel and threw it towards them.

'This breakfast better be worth all this,' Navjyot muttered as she watched Meera roll over to her sister.

'Who makes kids play a game for food? This is like one of those dystopian novels I love to read but would hate to live through,' Anika said.

'Now what?' Bubbles asked as they watched the twins scuttle across the ladder to the green flag which they touched. For a heart-stopping moment they just stood there and watched the three of them, and Anika was sure they were going to leave them stranded in the middle of the field. But she saw them exchange a look with each other before reaching down for the ladder, lifting it up and flipping it over so that it landed close to their huddle.

'Okay. Do you think we can all make it over?' asked Navjyot, 'We'll have to take a long leap right at the end.'

Anika looked at Bubbles with concern. 'What do you think?'

Bubbles nodded silently.

The twins were waving at them frantically. 'You only have a minute left! Hurry!' one of them screeched.

'Anika, you go with Navjyot, I'll come at the end,' Bubbles said, and even though Anika had her doubts about the idea, she and Navjyot scuttled across the ladder to the end and then jumped clean across, landing next to the green flag.

'Bubbles, come on, you can do it!' Anika shouted, waving her arms.

Anika watched as Bubbles's gaze swept across the field, taking in the dwindling chaos. Two teams were still making it across: one had four members and the other had five members intact.

As he began walking on the outer edges of the ladder, Anika was reminded of the exact same scene from her favourite fantasy trilogy, *The Necromancer of Nagasandra*. In it, the heroine, Tilakavati—who Anika always imagined looked exactly like her, even though the author described

her as a seven-foot-tall Amazon with washboard abs and an assassin's smile—had crossed an actual lava-filled chasm on a ladder, while a cat with snakes for tongues had chased her. Tilakavati's teacher, a monk called Than Nguyen who served up fiery soups with a side of wizardry, had taught her to master the inner storm with outer calm.

Anika thought that this might be useful advice for Bubbles and she yelled it out. But this seemed to confuse him and he stopped walking, and shut his eyes.

'You idiot!' she heard Mansi scream. 'Open your eyes and waaaaalk!'

'You can do it!' yelled Navjyot.

Anika watched as Bubbles opened his eyes and ran across the ladder as though he was in fact being chased by a cat with snakes for tongues. At the tip of the ladder, he threw his body through the air, arms and legs stretched out like Tilakavati, though he landed on his belly with a thud, sending up a massive cloud of dust.

'Did I make it?' he asked, face down on the ground, his voice muffled.

As the dust settled, Anika scanned the distance between him and the green flag and felt her heart sink.

7

Growing Girls Need Food!

VASU RUBBED HIS SLEEP-ENCRUSTED EYES and sat up in bed. After the long journey to TOMBE and the trauma of being abandoned by his parents, he'd fallen asleep immediately after they'd left. This was a rarity. Usually, he tossed and turned for a good couple of hours before sleep claimed him. When he'd woken up it was without the usual scratchy-itchy feeling in his eyes, and the fog of exhaustion that shrouded him. He'd actually felt rested.

Bubbles Sengupta was nowhere to be seen but he had clearly been in the room at night. From the looks of his unmade bed and pile of clothes that had been dumped on top of it, he was evidently not a tidy person.

Vasu's stomach rumbled, alerting him to the fact that he hadn't eaten since yesterday afternoon. He didn't particularly want to venture out, meet new people and eat with them, and debated staying in the safety of his cabin for a little longer. But when his stomach's protests refused to pipe down, he combed his hair and brushed his teeth in the attached bathroom, then stepped outside

to find some food. Only to discover that the camp wore a strangely deserted look. He wasn't a believer in 'the early worm catches the bird', but it couldn't have been that late, could it? Looking up and down the silent empty pathway, he was reminded of his favourite post-apocalyptic zombie multiplayer game, *Brain Dead Redemption*. But instead of the thrill he usually felt when he thought of it, a shiver went down his spine. What if everyone was gone because they *had* turned into zombies and were hiding inside the cabins and in the trees, waiting for him to come out so they could pounce on him and eat brain fry for breakfast? Made with *his* brains. The very thought of it forced his feet to speed up and he was soon jogging towards the single-storey building that had been pointed out as the 'cafeteria' the previous evening.

Vasu felt his body relax when he found the staff setting up the serving stations. He hoped there were sausages and omelettes for breakfast. Or some poori bhaji. Ooh, and he wouldn't mind some double-sided buttered toast and sweet, milky tea either.

Vasu went up to one of the staff members cautiously. He didn't have the rotting-flesh look of a zombie, but still, one could never be too sure.

Vasu stood a good foot away and smiled in what he hoped was a polite, please-don't-eat-me way. 'Good morning, Uncle,' he said. 'Can I have a cheese, mushroom and ham omelette please?'

The man looked Vasu up and down and smiled. 'Of course! Just give me a second. I'll get it for you right away!'

Vasu was just about to say 'thank you', when the man's face morphed into an expression of fury. 'Where do you think you are? THIS IS TOMBE! Not a five-star hotel!' he yelled.

Vasu shrank back in horror.

'I-I'm s-s-s-orry. I didn't mean to—' Vasu stuttered, as the man walked away and pushed open a door that read 'Staff Only'.

Vasu walked up to what looked like a platter of cutlets. A small card in front identified them as 'Spirulina and Moringa Cutlets with Activated Charcoal Relish'. What was moringa? And why were they feeding them coal for breakfast? Next to the platter was a large bowl of gloopy white yoghurt and a basin of something brown and clumpy, which the sign said was 'Horse Millet Porridge'.

Vasu picked up two cutlets, hoping that moringa tasted like chicken, when the doors of the cafeteria swung open and a swarm of sweaty, dirty and angry-looking campers wearing green tracksuits entered. Some were yelling, some were crying and some had an expression of complete misery on their faces.

'Losers will form a neat and orderly line here,' one of the counsellors barked. 'Winners can go and sit at the main table up in the front where they will be served breakfast.'

Vasu slipped the cutlets into his pocket and watched the children fall into line grumbling. He joined the end of the line, hoping no one would notice he wasn't in the tracksuit, which was unlikely given that he was wearing fire-engine red, monster truck pyjamas.

Vasu tried to blend in behind a tall girl with two long plaits, a plan that was foiled when two girls who confusingly looked alike pushed him out of the line and approached the tall girl.

'This is all your fault!' one of the girls hissed. 'If you hadn't insisted that that useless lump join us, we would have won. We would have been sitting at the winners' table!'

'Don't call him a useless lump!' said a very short girl.

'Why not? Is he your boyfriend?' sneered the first girl.

'No!'

'P-p-p-please don't fight. She's right. I'm the reason we lost!' a small, plump-faced boy pleaded, appearing next to the group. Lump was cruel, Vasu decided, but he *was* rather round.

'See! Even he knows what a loser he is. Remind us to never join your stupid team again,' one of the identical girls said. *Ah! Twins*, Vasu realized.

'Fine by us!' the short girl hissed. 'Right, Navjyot?'

'You're giving me a headache, Anika. Let's just have breakfast!'

Vasu filed their names away in his mind.

'Me? What did I do?' Anika asked, looking hurt.

'ENOUGH!' Navjyot snapped and then turned around to face the front of the line.

Anika kept grumbling under her breath about how unfair everything was, as the line shuffled forward.

When they reached the buffet Navjyot studied what had been laid out for them. She picked up a glass of green, murky-looking liquid and sniffed it, making a face.

'What is this?' she asked the counsellor suspiciously.

'Breakfast!'

Navjyot snorted. 'Right. Where's the rest of the breakfast?'

‘*This* is it.’ The counsellor smiled blandly.

‘No way! I need food. Real food. Eggs, toast, oats, upma. I need protein. Lots and lots of it.’

The counsellor seemed unfazed by the girl’s outburst and said in the most pleasant of voices, ‘If you wanted more to eat, you should have tried harder to win the game, don’t you think?’

‘I AM A GROWING GIRL! I NEED FOOD. I’m not a rabbit who can survive on green juice!’ Navjyot yelled, and the entire cafeteria fell silent, watching this mountain of a girl quiver in anger.

But her words triggered something in Vasu’s brain. *Rabbits! Oh no.*

‘Idiotidiotidiot,’ Vasu muttered.

‘Hey! Who are you calling an idiot?’ the girl named Anika asked.

‘Me! I’m an idiot. I totally forgot. I have to go.’

Vasu turned around and ran out of the dining hall. He ran the fastest he had ever run in his life. Faster than his Grade 2 sports day, in which he’d been dressed as a bunny. Faster than when he’d been chased by his neighbour’s cat through their home. Faster than the time he’d run home from the bus stop to download the latest weapons drop in *Brain Dead Redemption*. By the time he reached his cabin, he was very, very out of breath.

He dragged the chair right up to the wall next to his bed and clambered on top of it, and proceeded to remove the slatted panel fixed over a vent in the wall.

Vasu peered inside and called out, ‘Hello! Helloooo! Heeellllooooooo!’

He was so intent on what he was doing that he didn't hear the door to the cabin open or close.

But he did hear a perplexed voice ask, 'Umm. What are you doing?'

Vasu turned around to find the girl called Anika and the round-faced boy from the cafeteria standing at the entrance of the cabin and looking at him curiously.

'Is everything okay?' the boy asked.

'Anthrax!' Vasu shouted.

'What?' the two of them asked, looking confused.

'Anthrax!' Vasu yelled. 'I left Anthrax in there.'

Anika looked horrified. 'Who brings anthrax to camp? How do you even have anthrax?'

'What is anthrax?' asked the other boy.

'It's a deadly bacteria used as a biological weapon,' said Anika.

'No it isn't!' said Vasu.

'Yes it is!'

'It's my pet hamster!'

Anika, who had been backing away towards the door, stopped. 'Your what?'

'My pet hamster.'

Anika pursed her lips. 'You named your pet hamster Anthrax?'

'Yes,' said Vasu.

'And you brought him to camp?'

'*Her*. Gender biased much?' snapped Vasu.

This seemed to annoy Anika greatly, but the boy seemed delighted by this information.

'You have a pet hamster? I've always wanted a pet, but my parents keep saying that I am too irresponsible to have one. May I please meet Anthrax?'

Vasu looked up at the hole in the wall.

'You left her inside that vent?' asked Anika. 'Who does that?'

'I put her inside last night. I heard some of the counsellors talk about doing a bag check. I didn't want them to take her away. And then I forgot I'd put her there and left for breakfast!'

Vasu hoisted himself up again and looked inside the vent.

'Anthraaaaax!' Vasu crooned. 'Come to Daddyyyy.'

He could hear Anika snigger behind him, but ignored her.

'Anthrax?' he called and put his hand inside the vent and waved the cutlet about. 'Daddy has brought breakfast! Come get it!'

When he still couldn't hear the little pitter-patter of Anthrax's feet he felt tears prick his eyes.

'Where is she? Can I meet her?' he heard the boy call from below.

'She's gone!' Vasu wailed.

'Gone? Where could she have gone?' asked Anika.

The grate didn't cover a single square hole in the wall as he'd thought last night. He had been so tired he hadn't checked it properly. It covered a long, dark tunnel.

A tunnel that Anthrax had wandered off down.

8

100 Vitamins for Breakfast

'MISS KAUR, I CAN SEE why you were referred to us for discipline and anger issues. Your behaviour at breakfast was unacceptable,' murmured Dr. Basith.

Navjyot glared at the woman seated across from her.

Dr. Basith looked like a model. She was tall, slender and had the kind of skin the women on the face creams her mother bought had. It glowed. Her hair was a tumultuous mix of auburn, orange and blonde and was pulled into a high ponytail that curled over her right shoulder like a sleek and slinky snake.

'I—'

'She wasn't done speaking, Miss Kaur!' Dr. Kiran admonished as he entered the room. 'Tut-tut, I see we must teach you some basic manners as well!'

Dr. Basith's red lips stretched into a smile. 'We have much work to do with you here at TOMBE. Your parents were right to send you to us. How can a sportsman such as yourself hope to reach the highest levels of excellence and success

with such low mental fortitude? Discipline of the mind is so important, so, so important. And you have none of it. You must control your emotions. You must not let them control you.'

'Sports*person*,' Navjyot said through gritted teeth. She knew she should just shut up and let this horrible woman say whatever she wanted, but unfortunately, Navjyot was not built that way. She always had to say exactly what she was thinking. It was what had landed her here in the first place.

'Excuse me?' Dr. Basith asked, her eyes narrowing even further.

'Sportsperson. I'm not a sports*man*, I'm a sportsperson.'

'Let's not get sidetracked by semantics now, Miss Kaur,' Dr. Basith said. 'Your reaction to the meal offered in the dining hall today was uncalled for. We provide all inmates at TOMBE with a diet that has been specially designed and calibrated to their body's needs, *not* their wants. To not only turn your nose up at breakfast but also demand to be fed carbohydrates and fat!' She shuddered delicately as though repulsed by the very idea.

Navjyot thought that if she gritted her teeth any further they would turn to dust.

'Miss Kaur, I know you *think* you need upma and toast and parathas for breakfast. My body used to crave those things too,' Dr. Kiran said. 'But then I saw how they were weighing me down. Literally! How they dulled my brain. My reflexes. These days, my breakfast is a carefully calibrated intake of 100 vitamins and supplements and I have never felt or looked better. See!' He flexed his left bicep.

'Your parents signed a form stating that you would adhere to all the rules of TOMBE. That includes following the strict diet that has been set out for you. What you so contemptuously dismissed as rabbit food was cutting-edge nutrition that is going to revolutionize the world!' Dr. Kiran added.

Dr. Basith smiled at Navjyot encouragingly, as though waiting for her to respond. Navjyot wanted to tell both of them what they could do with their cutting-edge nutrition and 100 vitamins, but her stomach spoke instead and emitted a loud rumble.

'Please, I'm hungry. I just want to eat some food. Please,' she whispered.

'I'm glad you know the word "please".' Dr. Basith smiled. 'It shows some hope for you, however miniscule. Now, let's try and make some more progress.' She pressed a small buzzer on her table and the door to the room opened. A counsellor entered carrying a tray with a tall glass of green juice.

Navjyot felt a sinking sensation in her stomach as she watched the counsellor place the tray on the table.

'Since you felt the juice we offered you was so meagre, here's a bigger serving. I'm sure you'll find this more substantial and to your liking,' murmured Dr. Basith.

'You know what to do!' Dr. Kiran said, nodding at the glass.

Navjyot stared at it.

'I don't think you want to find out what happens to those who don't do as they're told at TOMBE,' he added.

Navjyot was hungry. But she didn't want to give these two the satisfaction of drinking their dumb juice. But she also registered the threat implied in Dr. Kiran's words.

‘I don’t have all day, Miss Kaur. Time is a-ticking!’ he trilled. But there was an edge to his words.

A sudden scuttling noise echoed in the room. Navjyot thought she was the only one who heard it, but she saw Dr. Basith’s head shift a fraction of an inch at the sound. She then shook her head and turned her attention back to Navjyot.

Navjyot took a small step forward.

She heard the scuttling sound again. It wasn’t coming from inside the room though, but somewhere outside. This time it was accompanied by a squeak.

‘What was that?’ Dr. Basith asked.

‘It sounded like a rat!’ Navjyot said.

‘Don’t be ridiculous, we got rid of all rats in Sector 2—’ she stopped when Dr. Kiran glared at her. ‘We do not have rats at TOMBE!’ Dr. Basith amended.

‘Any wild animals at TOMBE will be neutralized!’ the counsellor piped up.

There was another squeak. Dr. Basith ducked her head under the table as Dr. Kiran stood up abruptly from his chair. Navjyot scanned the room and her eyes came to rest on a slatted metal grate covering some kind of vent on the wall behind Dr. Basith’s desk. She could make out something white and fluffy behind it.

Dr. Basith unclipped a walkie-talkie from her belt and pressed a button before speaking into it, ‘Has there been another breach in Sector 2?’

Navjyot noted that the small, furry creature in the grate was too large to be a mouse and too fluffy to be a rat. She was trying to think of what it might be, when she saw a

larger, less furry, more human face appear next to it. Navjyot wondered if she was so hungry she was imagining things, when she realized it was the boy from breakfast that morning who'd been wearing the ridiculous red pyjamas.

Navjyot stayed exactly where she was, and watched as a massive grin broke out on his face, and a pair of hands scooped the fluffy thing up.

The creature squeaked again.

Dr. Basith shrieked into the phone. 'There is something on the loose! Find out what it is and exterminate it immediately.' When she slammed the phone down, she saw Navjyot staring behind her and began to turn around. Navjyot didn't think twice.

She leapt forward, picked up the tall glass of green juice and shrieked out a demented-sounding 'Cheers!' before downing it all in one go.

9

Seizures Are Best Controlled with a Nelson

'WHY'D YOU NAME HER ANTHRAX?' Bubbles asked Vasu as Anika tore off a tiny piece of a very squashed, very gross-looking moringa and spirulina cutlet and placed it in front of the hamster. They were all sitting around her on the bed in Vasu and Bubbles's room.

'Why'd your parents name you Bubbles?' retorted Vasu.

'Because I had a round, bubble-like face when I was born. And I guess I still do,' Bubbles said, self-consciously.

'Oh. Well I named her Anthrax after my second favourite weapon of choice in my most favourite video game, *Brain Dead Redemption*,' Vasu said.

Bubbles didn't think it was a very good reason but kept his opinion to himself. He had once told his neighbour Shailaja Aunty that her sambhar had too much asafoetida and she had stopped speaking to his mother for almost a month. Some people just didn't like hearing the truth.

Bubbles had worried and fretted after his cabinmate had disappeared through the hole in the wall. While a part of him knew it didn't make sense to worry so much about someone he hadn't even met properly, he couldn't help it. He was a worrier. And cooking was usually how he helped himself get over worrying. In an unpredictable world, Bubbles had learnt that finely dicing tomatoes, letting something simmer on a low flame for an hour or watching cookies rise in the oven were all excellent ways to quieten the chatter in his mind.

Anika prodded the bit of cutlet towards the hamster, who sniffed it once, twice and then turned away from it before falling asleep.

'Even *she* doesn't want to eat the food here,' Anika snickered. 'I don't feel so bad about not winning The Floor Is Lava if this is what the team that won got for breakfast.'

'Yeah, but everyone else got a glass of green juice,' said Vasu. 'How is that breakfast?'

'Exactly,' agreed Anika. 'My parents are ultramarathoning gym bunnies who have kale juice flowing through their veins. But even they eat eggs and have a smoothie in the morning.'

'Why did they send you here?' asked Bubbles. Anika seemed so confident, and the way she'd tackled the course this morning had been amazing.

'I guess because I don't look like the offspring of super athletes? I'm short, and chubby, and I'm not into sports the way they want me to be.' Ani shrugged, and looked down at her feet. 'I can't stick to any one thing either. I keep moving from one hobby to another. My parents say it's because I

have no grit and determination. But I don't understand why I have to focus on one thing *now*. Isn't the whole point of being a kid trying out a bunch of things?'

'Of course it is!' chimed in Bubbles.

'Ha! Look who's talking. I bet you've always known you want to be a chef.'

Bubbles smiled and stroked Anthrax's little head. He *did* want to be a chef, and had known that for a long, long time, but he didn't think that's what his parents wanted for him.

'Why are you here?' Ani asked Vasu, who grunted in response.

'I don't think Dr. Kiran's revolutionary camp solves grunting issues,' Ani responded.

Vasu stayed silent for a bit and then let out a long sigh. 'My parents think I have an avoidant personality, that I don't want to engage with the real world, so I have immersed myself in make-believe, violent, multiplayer video games which I am addicted to. Happy?' And with that he scooped up Anthrax, went over to his bed and lay down with his back towards them.

Ani shot Bubbles a 'what's with him?' look, but he just shrugged in response.

'I know it's probably not a great idea to talk about food when we haven't eaten anything but green juice all morning, but tell me about your YouTube channel?' Anika asked Bubbles.

Bubbles felt a warm feeling spread through his chest. No one but his Dida ever asked him about his YouTube channel. Even his parents who had initially supported it as a hobby now thought it was a digital pathway to destruction.

'It's called Breakfast with Bubbles, and I make my favourite breakfast items from around the world, but with a twist.'

'Not a healthy twist, right?' asked Ani suspiciously. 'You aren't here researching for the channel, are you?'

'No, no! I flip key ingredients in the recipe with something else that alters the taste of the final dish.'

'Like cabbage payasam?'

Bubbles gagged at the idea of cabbage payasam. How could anyone even think of such a monstrosity?

Ani leaned forward and dropped her voice to a whisper. 'My mom made it one Diwali a few years ago. And she kept going on and on about a secret, healthy ingredient, and made us all try and guess what it was. No one guessed cabbage for obvious reasons. I couldn't stand the sight of it for months afterwards.'

They both giggled and Bubbles was about to tell Anika about the rather amazing black rice payasam he'd once eaten on vacation when the door to their cabin slammed open with such force that he was sure there would be a door shaped imprint on the wall.

Navjyot stood there, the light streaming around her head like a halo, making her look like a tall, angry angel with two very long braids.

'Hi Navjyot!' Anika chirped. 'Is everything okay?'

Vasu sat up in his bed and stared at them.

Navjyot stalked into the room and planted herself right in front of him. 'No. Everything's not okay! I had to drink leaf mulch because *he* was crawling around looking through vents with some kind of stunted Shih Tzu.'

'Who are you calling a stunted Shih Tzu?' Vasu yelled.

'Where is it? Where are you hiding it?'

'I don't know what you're talking about!'

'Don't act all innocent. I saw a white fluffy thing through the vent and then I saw your face. Dr. Basith was going to call pest control to flush you out and then I saved your butt by drinking the juice. You owe me an answer.'

'I don't owe you anything,' Vasu insisted 'Who do—'

Vasu was cut off as his entire body started quivering and his face turned red before he broke into hysterical giggling.

'Is this funny to you?' Navjyot asked

The three of them stared as Vasu began to writhe and contort.

'I think he's having a seizure!' said Anika.

'What do we do?' Bubbles fretted.

'I'm going to tackle him!' Navjyot said decisively and began to advance towards Vasu with a determined look on her face.

'She's a state-level wrestler!' Ani told Bubbles, and he wondered why a five-foot-nine-inch tall, solid wall of muscle was at a camp like TOMBE.

'It's okay, little friend,' Navjyot said softly to Vasu as she took another step forward, 'I'm not going to hurt you!'

This seemed to get Vasu's attention and he started to hop away from her, shaking his head vigorously. When she was just a few inches away from him, he yelled out, 'Wait!'

'Why?' asked Navjyot, inching closer. She looked like she was almost enjoying the idea of tossing the boy to the ground. She looked at Ani and Bubbles over her shoulder. 'If I get him into a Nelson then we can contain and immobilize him!'

'A what?' asked Bubbles.

'A Nelson. Look I don't have time to explain this to you, just watch!' And with that Navjyot lunged at Vasu who screamed and then rather elegantly ducked under her arms and ran to the other side of the room.

'Wait! Wait! I'm not having a seizure. It's Anthrax.'

Navjyot spun around on her feet, with an incredulous look on her face. 'How did you do that? I haven't had wrestling practice for three days and I'm getting beaten already!' she wailed.

Vasu unzipped his hoodie and Anthrax's small head popped out.

'Aha, I knew it! A stunted Shih Tzu,' yelled Navjyot triumphantly.

'Calm down!' Bubbles yelled louder. 'Anthrax is a hamster. Not a rat, a mouse, or a stunted Shih Tzu. A hamster. Now sit down.'

Navjyot, surprised that the small round boy had it in him to yell at her like that, smiled in disbelief and obeyed.

10

Not Your Typical Curd Rice

ANIKA WIGGLED ABOUT TILL SHE felt comfortable sitting in padamasana, so that she could 'manifest' her ideal future self.

A counsellor named Senalda was weaving in and out of the small group of campers gathered in a clearing called the Mindfulness Zone, which was right next to the army-style obstacle course they were forced to cry their way through every morning. Anika found this juxtaposition both hilarious and cruel and she'd pointed it out to a girl called Kiran sitting next to her. But the only response she'd gotten was a furrowed brow and a long sigh. Anika didn't think she'd ever say these words, but she missed Navjyot, who was in a different mid-morning group that day.

Senalda went up to her own yoga mat at the front and sat down.

'Now, remember it's important to be comfortable in the way you're sitting. You can't manifest if you're not in sync with how your body feels. I'm going to sit in padmasana, because my body, which is lean and muscled, can do that.

Your bodies are, well, we know what your bodies are like. Let's see if you can all sit cross-legged first.'

Horrible witch, Ani thought. Who did she think she was, implying their bodies were somehow 'less than' just because they didn't look a certain way? But Ani's scowl soon turned into an expression of delight as she watched Senalda's legs refuse to fold into lotus pose, her knees jutting out awkwardly.

Senalda glared at Ani, who smiled sweetly at her, before unfolding her legs from padmasana and then refolding them with ease.

'I guess what our bodies look like has nothing to do with how flexible they are, Senalda Ma'am!' Ani called out. 'Maybe *you* should try sitting cross-legged first?'

Ani turned to look at the other children, hoping to get at least one grin of approval, but all she got was stoic silence. On the one hand, she couldn't blame them. It had been four days since they'd arrived at TOMBE. Four days of 4 a.m. wake-up calls, followed by something called Wolf Breathing and LED light bathing, which involved them placing weird helmets which lit up from the inside on their heads, throwing deep red pulsing lights over their eyes. Anika was sure the helmets were scanning their brain waves or something but Navjyot had dismissed this as far-fetched. There were boot camp drills during which the counsellors screamed incessantly at them. 'Run like the enemy carbs are chasing you!' 'I've seen better coordination in a sack of potatoes!' and 'You're not tired—you're just lazy in disguise!' Then there was the food. The single glass of green juice they were served every morning for breakfast was foul tasting but—

and this was what Anika couldn't fully fathom—oddly filling. The other meals of the day *looked* more substantial but were just as gross: a steamed head of broccoli or cauliflower for lunch and a bowl of boiled mushrooms for dinner seemed to be what they were expected to eat for the duration of their imprisonment. These things were enough to crush anyone's soul, but Anika couldn't understand how most of the campers seemed to not only accept that this was their life at TOMBE, but also appeared to be largely okay with it. No one really complained or groaned or mumbled other than her and Navjyot. Bubbles was too sweet to, and despite their best efforts to include him, Vasu wanted very little to do with their group and spent as much time as he could by himself or with Anthrax. The latter was made difficult by Bubbles who wanted to hold, pet and tell bedtime stories to the hamster whenever he could. Something that Vasu didn't seem happy with at all.

But what Anika really hated were the games they were 'invited' to play. There was always only one prize: the promise of a meal that was better than everyone else's.

The game of Capture the Flag the previous day had become particularly vicious when word had gotten around that the winning team would get special dahi bhaat. After eating steamed vegetables and juice for three days the mention of possibly eating rice and curd had sent the campers into a frenzy and the evening air had been filled with surprised screams and grunts of pain as flags were captured, bodies were tackled and then imprisoned in makeshift jails. Navjyot had led their team of four to victory, even after Bubbles had sat paralysed with fear inside one

of the giant rubber tyres they were forced to flip across the obstacle course every morning. Ani's knee still throbbed from when Meera and Mansi tripped her over and Navjyot had lost a clump of hair when a girl from another team had grabbed hold of her shiny black locks to stop her from reaching for the flag. But they'd still been a winning team somehow.

The other campers had watched in silent rage as they'd marched up to the head table at dinner and sat down in front of dome-covered plates. Bubbles had whispered he didn't feel like he'd earned the prize, but Vasu had felt no such qualms. Even though he hadn't done much to contribute to their victory, he'd grabbed the dome and all but planted his face in the bowl of curd rice in front of him. Then his face had become all weird when the actual taste of it registered.

'Excuse me,' he'd asked a passing counsellor 'This doesn't taste like curd rice!'

The counsellor had smiled widely. 'Isn't it divine? It's made with llama milk curd! You don't have to thank us, but you're welcome!'

Vasu had gagged at this information and refused to eat the rest of his meal, but Ani would have eaten emu milk curd rice to avoid the usual bowl of shiitake mushrooms they'd had every night at dinner.

She now watched Senalda who was sitting in some twisted parody of padmasana, as she told the group how they were to manifest their goals.

'Okay, everyone, take a deep breath... in through your third eye, out through your heart chakra. I want you to visualize

your future self: successful, succinct and with 14 per cent body fat, free of the shackles of processed food. You're not chasing this person—they're chasing you, because they are desperate for you to be them. When you vibrate at your highest, most honest frequency, the universe will grant you this future self immediately. Think of it as same-day delivery for the soul.'

Ani pressed her lips together to stop herself laughing. This woman couldn't be serious. Once again, she looked around her, but everyone else seemed to be sitting with their eyes closed, imagining their future, fat-free selves running towards them.

Ani still couldn't get a handle on what TOMBE's deal was. It was part extreme physical endurance, part hocus-pocus self-help, a whole lot of steamed vegetables, freezing cold showers and a gross ritual of using something called a neti pot to rinse mucus out of their nasal cavity.

Dr. Kiran and Dr. Basith weren't always there, but somehow Ani was convinced they were always watching them, even though she couldn't find a single security camera no matter how hard she looked.

Senalda's annoying horsey voice called out, 'Open your eyes, everyone! When you go back to your cabins, remember to use your Imaginate Innovate Activate Diaries to record exactly what you saw in your manifestation, and maybe draw an image of the future you, running towards you!'

The group got up, some with more difficulty than others. Senalda herself seemed to be unable to untangle herself so Ani put aside her intense dislike for the woman and headed over to her and extended a hand. The counsellor looked as

though she wanted to swat it away but then she gave in and took her assistance.

'You're welcome!' Ani said sweetly, even though Senalda hadn't thanked her, and began walking back to her cabin. Just then, a familiar trumpeting music played over the PA system. Ani felt her heart sink. It could only mean one thing.

'Inmates, assemble in the play arena! It is time for the next TOMBE game! Inmates, assemble in the play arena! You have five minutes.'

11

A Rather Insulting Treasure Hunt

VASU WAS EXPERIENCING THE HUMILIATION of having his daily readings taken when the campers were summoned for that day's game. He wasn't sure if he was relieved or upset. On the one hand he detested having to go and play these stupid games in stupid teams for stupid prizes. On the other hand, having his weight recorded, being forced to pee in a cup and stick his tongue out every morning was the stuff of nightmares. There was a digital band that had been welded around his wrist which was scanned by a consistently cheerful counsellor called Dev who then gave him some vitamins in a cup.

As always, Vasu spat the vitamins out the minute he left the medical bay where all campers were required to come in for daily 'data gathering'. He shoved them into the soil of a potted plant. What did they need so much data for anyway? Vasu had attended residential camps before, and TOMBE was nothing like them. For one, he'd never been asked to pee in a cup, and

two, the games they conducted in the other camps didn't have the dark, sinister edge the ones they played here did.

Vasu saw Anika, Navjyot and Bubbles bearing down the pathway, no doubt looking for him so that they could all be 'a team' and participate in whatever fresh hell the counsellors had cooked up for the game of the day. He turned right around and tried to hide behind a tree but then he heard Bubbles call out his name. The boy was hell bent on them being friends, and even after Vasu had shared his entire 'I'm a lone wolf' theory with him he refused to take the hint. Plus, he liked Anthrax a little too much, and was always bringing her things to eat that he'd foraged from the gardens of TOMBE or telling her stories or making up songs for her. Anthrax was *his* hamster. She and Vasu didn't need new friends. They didn't need *any* friends. They were happy just as they were, thank you very much. Well, not happy because obviously they were in TOMBE. But they were fine. Okay-ish. Normal. Whatever.

'Hey!' Vasu heard Navjyot call out as he ducked behind a tree, 'We can see you Vasu! Get over here right now.'

Vasu let out a very un-Archer-Babylon-like shriek, as Bubbles's round face popped up right next to him behind the tree. 'Hi! Shall we go play?'

'Do I have a choice?' grumbled Vasu.

'No! Now move!' Ani ordered.

Vasu wasn't sure how he'd gotten lumped with two bossy girls, but when he saw the other campers, like Meera and Mansi, he realized it could have been much, much worse. Vasu dragged his feet and dawdled, and as a result they were the last to arrive.

Vasu was surprised to see that alongside Dr. Basith and the usual gang of TOMBE groupies—which is what he called the counsellors in his head—stood Dr. Kiran. Vasu hadn't seen that much of the camp founder since the orientation evening, though he had heard Navjyot talk about a lecture he'd given a group she'd been in, on 'biohacking to cheat death'. Apparently, Dr. Kiran went everywhere with a team of scientists who tracked and monitored and tested him constantly. His goal, he'd shared with the campers, was to not die.

'Good morning TOMBErs!' Dr. Kiran's voice boomed over the microphone. Everyone winced and shuffled as the speakers screeched. 'I am so pleased to see how all of you are blooming at TOMBE. When I was your age, all I did was sit inside my room and eat instant noodles and study. I didn't have the marvellous opportunity you all do to learn from the world's healthiest, smartest and most tested man. That's me, by the way! I'm forty-seven years old, but I have the heart of a thirty-three-year-old, the lungs of a twenty-one-year-old, and the metabolism of an eighteen-year-old. I have reversed ageing. I have! Mark my words, I will live forever. I will! My birthday only comes every eighteen months instead of twelve – that's six extra months a year, for free. Don't you want more free time? And I want to share that knowledge with you. The question isn't *if* it's possible—the question is whether you're willing to put in the work to *make* it possible.'

'How can his birthday come every eighteen months? That doesn't make any sense,' whispered Navjyot.

Vasu was confused too. He was turning thirteen next month, so if he had to reverse age like Dr. Kiran, then he would be... minus five years old?

Dr. Kiran had been pacing up and down as he spoke and he stopped in front of a girl with curly pigtails.

'You, young lady. Are you ready to put in the work?'

'I-I guess?' she stuttered.

'Guess? Why are you guessing? Commit yourself to the magical transformation I'm offering you. Don't you want to be peak-performance you? Is this,' he asked, gesturing towards her face and body, 'the best you can be?'

'N-no?' the girl ventured.

'What's wrong with how she is?' asked Ani.

'Shhhhhh!' hissed Vasu.

'The question we should all be asking is, what's right with it?' Dr. Basith countered.

'She looks fine to me!' Ani said. Vasu groaned. This girl and her need to have an opinion about everything. It was exhausting.

'Yeah!' Navjyot chimed in. 'And what's so great about how you look? Or how any of your counsellors look?

Dr. Kiran, rather than being upset by this back talk, seemed utterly delighted and actually clapped his hands in glee.

'We'll revisit this conversation at a later time. Now, I hear that Dev's team has organized a wonderful game for all of you today. The winners will get to taste my soon-to-be-launched nut pudding under the Dr. 4K Power Blaster Food Range.'

He paused as though expecting everyone to erupt into cheers and screams of excitement, but after eating moringa cutlets and llama milk curd rice, people had the obvious sense to be a little wary of whatever this nut pudding was. Vasu wished the games were optional, but they weren't. He'd asked.

Counsellor Dev bowed deeply to Dr. Kiran, before straightening to announce that they would be playing 'TOMBE Treasure Hunt'.

'Each team can come up and collect their first clue now.'

Navjyot pushed Vasu forward. 'Go on!'

Vasu didn't know why he always ended up listening to her but he went and picked up a chit from the upturned and slightly greasy-looking hat that Dev was holding out. He went back to the others, opened the folded piece of paper and read aloud from it.

'You huffed and you puffed, but you're just not that fit. Your next clue is waiting at the place where you quit.'

'That's mean!' Ani said.

'Where did we quit?' asked Vasu.

'The running track around the activity field!' said Bubbles. 'No one but Navjyot could finish it yesterday.'

'He's right. Let's go,' said Navjyot and the three of them turned around and ran in the direction of the field.

Vasu dragged his feet as he walked behind them. He wanted nothing more than to sit these dumb games out, but he'd seen how the counsellors treated the kids who didn't participate with enough 'enthusiasm'. What they made them do. Extra push-ups at the morning boot camp. Cruel taunts about why their parents had sent them to TOMBE. Halving the portions of steamed mushrooms at dinner. Which maybe wasn't the worst thing, considering how disgusting they tasted.

Their group reached the running track that encircled the activity field, sweat slithering down their backs. The morning sun was out in full force that day, and Vasu thought of how he

had planned to spend his summer in an air-conditioned room playing enough *Brain Dead Redemption* to put him on the league tables. He wondered where it had all gone so wrong.

'Okay, we're here now, but where do we look for the next clue?' asked Navjyot.

'Let's start at that table!' Ani said.

To the side of the track sat a desk and chair on top of which was a clipboard, with a list of the names of campers who had done the training course that morning, their timings and comments next to their names.

Parikshit: 9 minutes. Incomplete. Core strength of an amoeba.

Suma Bala: 14 minutes. Hand-eye coordination of a blind snake.

'But snakes don't have hands!' said Bubbles.

'Yeah, that's kind of the point they're making, Einstein!' snapped Vasu.

'I hate the counsellors. Why are they so mean?' asked Ani.

'Well, if they crush our spirits, then we're easier to manage,' said Navjyot. 'It's kind of like what my coach does back home. He insults everyone so much they just keep trying harder and harder for his approval and mind less and less what he's saying.'

Navjyot paused and cleared her throat, as though surprised she'd shared so much, then went back to rifling through the papers. She made a triumphant sound and pulled out a chit of paper.

'We said "portion control"—you said "double it". You better think before you eat another chicken nugget.'

'There are chicken nuggets here? WHERE?' whined Bubbles.

'Maybe that's the prize. Chicken nuggets!' said Ani, licking her lips at the thought of them.

Vasu huffed. *Idiots.* 'No way. You think they're going to feed us nuggets? The prize will probably be something disgusting like steamed banana peels.'

All their faces blanched. 'Okay, let's go to the cafeteria. The next clue has to be there,' Ani said.

They were met at the entrance of the cafeteria by Meera and Mansi and their sneering faces.

'Well, look who's here. The Fumbling Four!' said Meera. Or was it Mansi?

Navjyot took a threatening step towards them, and they scurried away down a corridor to the back, one of them yelling 'Stay back, giant freak!' over her shoulder.

'Okay, we're going to split up. Two of us will search behind the serving counters and two of us will check under each and every dining table in the room,' Navjyot told them.

Vasu began to feel frustrated as their search turned nothing up. If this were *Brain Dead Redemption*, he could summon an animated cerebellum that would offer to help him find out where the extra ammo he needed was hidden.

Suddenly, a loud crashing sound came from somewhere inside the cafeteria, followed by a blood-curdling scream.

'What was that?' whispered Ani.

God, please don't let it be a zombie, Vasu thought.

'I-I think we should leave,' Bubbles said.

But Navjyot was already running towards the screaming instead of away from it, and the other two followed. Not wanting to be left alone, Vasu reluctantly went after them and then he heard even more screaming, this time from

Ani. The three of them were standing in the middle of the corridor, horror etched across their faces.

At the door of the pantry were Mansi and Meera in their identical green tracksuits. Covered entirely in blood.

12

The Forbidden Snacks Society

NAVJYOT WATCHED IN DISGUST AS Mansi swept a finger through the blood coating her sister's face, put it in her mouth and licked it.

'It needs salt!' said Mansi.

Ani and Bubbles gagged next to her and Vasu was probably already puking in the corridor. For all his posturing and bragging about zombies and Archer-whats-his-name, he was a bit of a puski.

Meera laughed at their faces and nudged her sister. 'Mmmm, still feeling hungry, Mansi?'

'I sure am! I could use some fresh brains,' she replied and started to walk towards them.

'All work and no play makes Meera a dull girl,' Meera droned as she followed her sister.

Navjyot felt Vasu before she saw him. He had thrown himself in front of their small group, arms outstretched. 'Step back. I have experience killing zombies.'

'What are you doing? They're not zombies,' Navjyot said as she reached out and swiped some of the red liquid off

Meera's hand and licked it. 'It's not brains or blood. It's tomato puree.'

'Oh,' said Vasu and she could see he felt stupid about the whole thing. It *was* stupid, but also kind of sweet.

'But thank you for coming to our rescue,' Navjyot added.

Vasu's face twisted in embarrassment.

The twins were giggling, but Navjyot ignored them and turned around to face the others.

'Right, seeing that there's nothing in that room but puree, and we haven't found anything in the cafeteria, maybe we should go look somewhere else,' said Ani.

'Where?' asked Bubbles, as they stepped out of the cafeteria, surveying the perfectly manicured lawns.

'I remember seeing a door marked "Provisions" on the way to the data collection centre this morning. We could go look there?' asked Vasu.

'Good idea!' Navjyot responded. She was tired and despondent, but she wanted to make him feel better after his failed attempt at rescuing them from the twins. 'We have nothing to lose except the chance to eat Dr. 4K Power Blaster Nut Pudding!'

'Lead the way,' Ani told Vasu.

Vasu began to walk down the path, but not before Navjyot noted the small smile of pleasure on his face.

'Okay, so we go straight then right then left,' he said.

'Right,' said Bubbles.

'No left.'

'No. He meant right like riiiiight. Not right, right,' Ani said.

'Right!' said Bubbles.

'But I just said we have to go left!'

Navjyot was beginning to get a headache.

'Just keep going, and we'll follow you,' she said.

'Fiiiine! Don't get all snappy about it,' Vasu grumbled. He stopped at a fork in the pathway, and scrunched his forehead before yelping, 'I think it's this way!'

'You think?' asked Ani.

'No, I'm pretty sure. Yep, it's this way,' Vasu said and walked around one of the cabins and down a small slope before they came to a squat, ugly-looking concrete building that was set apart from everything else.

'What were you doing down here this morning?' asked Bubbles.

'I was trying to avoid going for data collection and lost my way,' admitted Vasu, walking up to the door marked 'Provisions'.

'Wait! What if someone is inside?' cautioned Ani.

'So? We're looking for the treasure hunt clues, not robbing the place. Why shouldn't we be here?'

'I don't know, I just feel like we're going to get into trouble,' said Ani.

'Tilakavati wouldn't worry about getting into trouble,' Vasu said snarkily. Navjyot didn't have it in her to listen to the two bicker again about who was better: Tilakavati or Archer Babylon. In fact, she never wanted to hear about either of those stupid characters again.

Vasu smirked when Ani didn't have a comeback and turned the door handle. It opened with an easy click and he looked at Ani as though to say 'See?'.

He pushed the door open and stepped inside. The others followed and looked around the room. There were boxes

stacked from floor to ceiling marked with labels like: 'jaggery' 'agar agar' and 'salt'.

'Why's there tomato puree and salt at this camp if we can't eat either of them?' asked Navjyot, opening a box and looking inside. She walked up to another row of cartons and ran her finger down the side: millets, moringa, mushrooms. Another box was taped shut and the words 'For Transfer to Sector 2' were written on the top in bold, red letters. *Where have I heard about Sector 2 before?* Navjyot wondered, pulling the box towards her and even before she opened it, a familiar smell assailed her nostrils. Cardamom and toasted almond slivers.

There was only one thing in the world that smelled this good. She ripped open the box and saw a familiar stainless steel dabba and whooped with joy! Prising open the lid she saw them.

Her mother's laddoos.

'Look! Look here,' she called out, rummaging through the box. Inside it were the snacks and treats that had been confiscated from the campers on the evening they'd arrived.

'My Twizzlers!' shrieked Ani, reaching in and grabbing the packet of candy.

There were other boxes marked for transfer to Sector 2, and Bubbles and Vasu opened one each, revealing a treasure trove of all the delicious, forbidden snacks they'd been denied since their arrival.

'Are you thinking what I'm thinking?' asked Ani.

'That we forget looking for the next clue and eat some snacks?' asked Vasu.

'Yessssss!' Ani hissed and proceeded to tear open the packet of Twizzlers and shove the contents in to her mouth.

'Only take what's yours! Don't eat anyone else's snacks, okay?' said Navjyot.

'Yes, Miss!' sniped Vasu, rummaging around till he found a packet of Scottish Shortbread. He fell to the floor and carefully opened the box before putting one of them in his mouth and groaning in ecstasy. Navjyot bit into a laddoo and felt intense longing. She missed her mother *so* much.

Navjyot watched Bubbles pick up a packet of something called nimki and stare at it.

'What's wrong, Bubbles?'

'Should we be eating these?' he asked.

Anika jumped in with a response as always. 'They're ours, why shouldn't we eat them?'

'It's not allowed, no? They took them from us for a reason.'

'That's right! They took them from us because they are horrible, bad people. Look, you can take a small taste of your forbidden snack,' Ani said 'You are a founding member of The Forbidden Snacks Society!'

Navjyot rolled her eyes. 'The what?'

'The Forbidden Snacks Society! We're a secret gang that searches for hidden, forbidden snacks and then eats them.'

'Why don't we just call it The Secret Snacks Gang then?' asked Vasu.

'Because my name sounds fancier and better. Like a secret society in an adventure novel,' huffed Anika. 'Eat your nimki, Bubbles. Salt tastes so good! And sugar!' she added, groaning.

Bubbles watched the three of them tuck in before opening his own packet of snacks. A calm and companionable silence settled over them.

Navjyot stood up and walked over to the boxes and peered at the candy, biscuits, power bars, bhujia and murukku inside and lifted the flap.

'Why do you think they're sending all this to Sector 2?' she asked.

'So we wouldn't find it and eat it? Guess they're too late!' Ani said cheerfully, actually licking the insides of the Twizzlers packaging. *Gross.*

'Now I remember! You know the day I was sent to Dr. Basith's office, after we played The Floor is Lava? When they heard Anthrax in the vent? They thought it was a breach in Sector 2. We've been here for almost a week now, and I haven't seen anything that says Sector 2. Have you?'

Navjyot waited for the others to answer but they were all busy eating, except Anika, who was looking longingly at Bubbles's packet of snacks.

'Hey! Did you hear what I said?' asked Navjyot, a little louder.

'Yes. Blah-blah-Sector 2-blah-blah. Happy?' asked Vasu. 'Look, we found a stash of snacks that can keep us going until we're released from TOMBE. Why should any of us care about Sector 2?'

Anika nodded in agreement, while Bubbles looked unsure of how to react. This made Navjyot forget her exhaustion. If there was one thing she couldn't stand it was a go-with-the-flow, let's-not-shake-anything-up-as-long-

as-things-are-working-out-for-us attitude. It sucked. She couldn't bear the status quo and hated being told to not care about something.

'Aren't you curious about what's in Sector 2? What's inside it that Dr. Basith wants neutralized? What if there's something there that tells us more about TOMBE? These weird bands they never let us take off, the daily data collection, the uniforms, the games! Who runs a camp like this? Don't you think we deserve to know more?'

'I'm thinking I can see why you're such a headache for your coach,' Vasu said. 'Don't you ever leave anything alone?'

Navjyot felt a white-hot rush of anger and stood up and stalked over to him. 'No, I don't leave things alone. Especially things that are unfair and wrong. People like you are the reason bad things happen, because you see them happening but don't do anything about it!'

Bubbles stood up. 'Please don't fight. Please?'

'We can't always just be nice, Bubbles,' Navjyot snapped. 'Stop being such a people pleaser. It's so fake.'

She felt awful when she saw his face fall, but he brushed off her hand when she reached for him and went and sat at the other end of the room.

'So what do you suggest we do? Knock on Dr. Basith's office door and ask her? Or even better, let's go find out from Dr. Kiran,' suggested Vasu with a smirk on his face.

'I am not suggesting that, *idiot*!'

'Then what?'

'I'm suggesting we find out where Sector 2 is and see for ourselves what's there.'

13

Everyone Has Drunk the Kool-Aid

VASU WAS A BUNDLE OF synonyms: he was upset, irate, irritated and annoyed.

'Let's not forget aggrieved,' Anika suggested.

'Yes! I am aggrieved! I don't want to forage in the forest at night. What if we eat a poisonous mushroom? Or get bitten by something? Or lose our way home? Or break our ankles and we can't move and then we have to eat each other one by one to stay alive till help arrives? My teeth aren't strong enough to chew through human muscle. WHAT WILL WE DO?'

'Look, I know I said we're The Forbidden Snacks Society, but we draw the line at cannibalism ok? We are *not* going to have to eat each other,' Ani said, rolling her eyes.

Vasu watched as she quickened her pace, Bubbles struggling to keep up with her, as they headed to the dispersal point for the latest game they had been summoned to play.

'We are not going to eat anything poisonous or human. And the chances of everyone breaking their ankles at the same time are unlikely,' Navjyot said in a soothing tone.

'Do you think we will find anything about Sector 2 in the forest?' asked Bubbles.

'Shh! Not so loud,' Navjyot whispered. 'Look, Sector 2 exists, but there's no mention of it anywhere in TOMBE. So it's obviously something they want kept secret. And what better place to conceal a secret location than a forest?'

Vasu wanted to argue that some secrets were best left alone and that forests were also great places to bury meddling kids who didn't know how to mind their own business. That they had somehow gotten through nine days of TOMBE was a miracle. There were less than two weeks left before they could all go back to their lives and reach level 4 of *Brain Dead Redemption* and cosplay as Archer Babylon at the next ZombieCon.

Earlier that evening, Vasu had finished attending a lecture on the links between micronutrients and mind power, when the loudspeakers had invited all inmates to assemble at the amphitheatre for information about the game of the day.

From where they were seated Vasu had an excellent view of the stage that was set below where Dr. Basith and Dr. Kiran, were as usual surrounded by counsellors. Vasu noticed for the first time just how ripped some of the counsellors were, but it wasn't just their bulging biceps and broad shoulders that caught his eye; it was the slightly menacing glint in their eyes that was always present. Especially when they were doing boot camp. Behind them was another group of counsellors, but they were smaller in size and more normal-looking.

Also, they had a slight air of nerdiness to them. These were the counsellors who collected their data every morning or took them through visualizations and manifestations. They weren't mean, but they weren't friendly either. They were just there.

'Welcome, campers!' Dr. K.K.K. Kiran said, his arms spread wide open. 'I trust your stay with us at TOMBE has so far been a journey of learning and self-discovery!'

'Are we inmates or campers? I wish he'd make up his mind!' huffed Anika.

Vasu *had* discovered some things about himself, which he would never admit to his parents. He didn't miss his video games as much as he expected to. And he liked writing his feelings down in his journal, though he refused to call it an Imaginate Innovate Activate diary. It made him feel calmer, and he liked drawing the bullies in school as weird, slightly gross items of food. He'd imagined Soham as a sushi roll made of stinky socks, and Rohit had been turned into a tall glass of falooda with maggots at the bottom.

'We hope they've also gone a long way in fostering a sense of camaraderie amongst you and your fellow inmates!'

Vasu snorted. Camaraderie? If that was the vibe they'd been going for, then they'd missed by a mile. The games, if anything, had made the campers organize themselves into small factions that were suspicious of the other. No one knew when a new game would be announced, or what it would be, or where it would happen, and this made people snap out of the otherwise pall of gloom they existed in, and made them nervous and jumpy. All they knew was that at the end of each game, a slightly less terrible meal awaited those

who won. And this promise of tasting something other than mushroom and broccoli turned everyone a little feral when they played.

Vasu watched Dr. Basith step forward.

'Today you will be playing a very different kind of hide-and-seek in the forest. Backpacks have been left on your beds. They contain cutting shears, a pair of tongs, a torchlight and a large bag. The game is simple, go into the forest in your groups and look for this plant.'

Dr. Basith lifted a potted plant from the floor and held it up. It had large, floppy, fluorescent green leaves that were streaked in purple and pink held up by long thin stems. Each stem had thin, sharp-looking spines running along it.

'This gorgeous creature hides in the depths of the forest, often camouflaged by other weeds, growing around the base of the *Palaquium ellipticum*.'

'You must seek out these plants and use the cutting shears and tongs to gather as many as you can find and collect them in the bags provided. As always, a special breakfast awaits those who arrive back at camp with the maximum weight of plants! A laminated photograph of both the *Palaquium ellipticum* and the sample you must collect will be handed to each team at the dispersal point in the forest. Good luck, campers. Go forth and seek! Hidden treasures await!' she trilled.

After the stage had emptied out, the campers had walked to their cabins, and the PA system had blared out their instructions for the evening ahead on loop.

'TOMBE Inmates! Attention! Please go to your rooms and gather the backpacks we have left on your beds and assemble

in the amphitheatre in ten minutes. We invite you all to a fun-filled game of nighttime hide-and-seek. Do not carry anything else with you but the backpacks. Though you may wish to carry your wits with you too!' The voice snickered at this, and Vasu decided if he ever met the person to whom this voice belonged, he would go Archer Babylon on them and take them down.

'How is this safe? Asking us to play hide-and-seek in the forest at night with nothing but—' Vasu rummaged about in his backpack '—a pair of cutting shears, a pair of tongs, a giant plastic bag and a torch!'

'Instead of complaining, think of this as an opportunity,' Navjyot said.

'To what?'

'To find Sector 2!' Navjyot replied.

Even though Vasu had zero interest in finding Sector 2, he had spent the last couple of days trailing behind the other three searching for clues about what it was, or where it might be. He told himself that he was still a lone wolf, but even wolves had to hang out with the rest of the pack sometimes, however annoying they were.

They had started out by studying all the maps across TOMBE looking for any mention of Sector 2. Anika had casually asked some of the campers during breakfast if they'd been to Sector 2 and if they would recommend it like it was some trending holiday destination. She'd been met with blank stares all around. They had explored the many narrow pathways and hidden corners of the TOMBE campus in pairs during their Golden Hour—a time to reflect in silence on their 'pitiful attempts at mastery of self and ruminate on the

long journey ahead of them'—and come up with nothing. They had even gone back to the provisions room to see if there were any more clues there—and snacks—but the door had been locked.

Vasu felt his anxiety levels go up, but all around him, the other campers didn't seem particularly perturbed that they were being sent into the forest at night to collect some rando plant. Even Poongothai, a girl who had cried every morning at breakfast this past week, seemed to accept the evening's 'game' with a small smile on her lips.

'Why does everyone look so ... chill?' Vasu asked.

'I know, it's almost like they're looking forward to going and rooting around for what looks like a plant that might kill us,' Ani said. She turned to a boy called Chetan walking behind them. 'Hey,' she asked him. 'What do you think of the game?'

Chetan's smile grew wider. 'I'm elated at this opportunity to test the limits of my resilience, and am in no doubt that it will only make me a stronger, more disciplined citizen of our nation.'

'Awesome!' said Ani, before turning back to Vasu and whispering, 'It's official, everyone has lost their minds.'

'I guess everyone's been drinking the TOMBE Kool-Aid!' said Vasu.

'Everyone but us!' muttered Ani.

'There's Kool-Aid here?' asked Bubbles excitedly.

14

Fss! Fss! Fss! Fss!

AS SHE WALKED TOWARDS THE boundary wall of TOMBE with the others, Ani couldn't shake off the feeling that they were all being watched.

Bubbles nudged her and gestured nervously to the tall gates ahead that were flanked by the kind of watchtower she had only ever seen in movies about dinosaurs, escaping prisoners and the world coming to an end. Ani squinted trying to see through the windows at the very top of the tower and realized there was no one inside, which for some reason was even creepier.

As they passed through the gates, which had opened with the most awful groaning sound, and walked into the forest, Ani shivered, convinced that something horrible was going to jump right out of the trees and chase them. As though sensing her fear, Bubbles reached out and grabbed her hand and gave it a tight squeeze. She squeezed it back and then let her hand rest in his soft palm, reassured by its lack of nervous, clammy sweat.

'We should figure out our secret call in case we get lost, separated, get into trouble or want to alert the others,' she whispered.

'Good idea,' he said 'I think it should be Fss! Fss! Fss! Fss!'

Ani giggled. 'Why?'

'Because we're the Forbidden Snacks Society! The Fss! And there are four of us, so four times.'

Ani tested it out, 'Fss! Fss! Fss! Fss!' and Bubbles responded similarly.

After twenty minutes of walking, they arrived at a clearing of sorts in the forest and to Ani's surprise, the campers went and sat in neat rows without being asked to. As though they knew what was expected of them. Only she, Navjyot, Vasu and Bubbles stayed where they were in a small knot.

'Let's go join them?' Ani suggested, and they went and made up the last row.

'Why isn't anyone saying anything?' whispered Bubbles.

He was right. For a group of children in the woods alone in the late evening, there was a strange silence that had settled over them.

'Campers! Welcome to TOMBE Hide-and-Seek,' said Dev, a counsellor Ani and Vasu called Data Dev since his main role at TOMBE seemed to be logging their vitals every morning at the data collection centre. He held up large, laminated cards of the spiny plant and the funny-named tree.

'This is what you're all going to be seeking for this evening. It's a wondrous plant endemic to these hills and it grows at the foot of the *Palaquium ellipticum*. Each of you will get two hours to fill your bags. There's a whistle in your backpack that

you can blow on should you lose your way or hurt yourselves. If we hear it, we will come and find you.'

What does he mean if we hear it? thought Ani. *What if they don't hear it? Will they just leave us in the forest?*

There was a chorus of 'Yes, Sir' from the group.

Vasu turned to Ani. 'What if we pick something that looks like this but is actually some other plant that's poisonous and we break out into pus-filled boils that kill us slowly or leave hideous scars all over our bodies. What will we do then?'

Ani had expected Bubbles to worry and fret like this but not Vasu. And while she wanted to tell him that nothing like that would happen, what did she know? The natural world was filled with things that wanted to be left alone and had no qualms about putting humans in their place.

'Well, I guess pus-filled boils is better than being the victim of cannibalism?' Ani said, trying to lighten the mood, but the dark look on Vasu's face told her she hadn't succeeded.

Data Dev took out a giant digital clock and placed it in front of the group. 'Your time starts now,' he yelled. He pushed down on a button, and the 1:20:00 displayed on it immediately began to race backwards. The campers jumped to their feet and began to fan out with their torches and laminated cards ready.

As the unofficial head of the FSS—she figured that if she came up with the name, she should be in charge of their first adventure—Ani placed Vasu up front with a torch, Bubbles behind him, then herself, and finally told Navjyot to stand behind her. She felt safer knowing that Navjyot literally and figuratively had her back as they wandered down one of the pathways leading from the clearing they'd been in.

'What is this thing even called?' Ani asked as she studied the laminated photo of the plant in her hand. 'They never told us.'

'Look, I think I found one!' Vasu called from up front and they rushed towards him.

They all stood around the tree and focused their torches at its base. Ani held the photo next to it. The leaves were broad, flat and bright green, streaked in pink and purple, and the thin stems were lined with tiny, vicious-looking spines.

Bubbles reached out to pluck one but then drew his hand back quickly with a small *huff*.

'It poked me!' he said with his lower lip sticking out.

'That's why they gave us the cutting shears and tongs, genius,' said Vasu.

'Look! We're meant to be looking for Sector 2, not actually plucking these stupid things,' Navjyot said impatiently.

Vasu and Bubbles had already started clipping the plant, though. 'See, we have to head back to the campsite at some point, and if we return with an empty bag, they'll make things even worse for us. Remember what happened to the kids who didn't "fully participate" in Simon Says that day?' Ani said turning to Navjyot. She shuddered at the memory of the four campers asked to stand absolutely still in the butterfly garden of TOMBE for an hour, with every twitch and shift forcing the clock to be reset for all of them. 'If we have something in our bag at least we can say we lost our way looking for more plants,' argued Ani.

Navjyot pursed her lips and Ani tried to suppress a grin. She knew the older girl didn't like being bested with logical answers.

'Fine,' Navjyot muttered. They worked together clipping and plucking, the silence punctured every now and then by a sudden sharp intake of breath, a whimper and the occasional cuss word when someone's finger encountered a spine.

Another group stumbled on to their patch and Bubbles reared up at the sight of Meera and Mansi. 'This is our spot! Find your own!' he yelled, much to Ani's delight. She liked this feisty side of Bubbles that came out every now and then.

The twins looked like they wanted to say something back, but then they just shook their heads, gave him identical dirty looks before whirling around and herding their team down another path.

'Look, our bags are a little full,' Ani said. 'It's the right time to get going.'

'Okay, but which way do we go?' asked Bubbles.

They looked around, at each other and then finally at Navjyot.

'Why are you all looking at me?' she asked. 'I thought Ani was in charge of our little secret society?'

'Because this was your idea!' said Vasu.

'And you're the oldest!' added Bubbles.

'And the tallest!' Ani chimed in. 'And as the head of the Forbidden Snacks Society, I am making you chief navigator. So, which way do we go?'

Navjyot grimaced and muttered something about these being stupid reasons before turning to her right and shouting, 'Follow me!'

'Why are we going this way?' asked Ani as they went down a pathway.

'I thought I was in charge?' Navjyot retorted.

'No! I'm in charge. You're the chief navigator, remember?'

'Look, this pathway is worn and defined, as though people have used it again and again over a period of time. The others were rough and rocky, so this seemed like a good way to go.'

Ani nodded, and followed her friend trying to keep the fear roiling inside her in check. They'd been walking for about fifteen minutes when Navjyot whispered, 'Stop! Look!'

But Ani wasn't sure if she wanted to stop. She didn't want to look around and see where they were. She had spent the last 900 seconds with her eyes trained on the back of Navjyot's head. The growth around them was thick and dense, and even though there were no creepy sounds or howling animals, the silence was somehow even more unnerving. If they just kept moving then they would never have to stop and look and find a crazed killer hiding in the branches.

God. She was beginning to sound like Vasu. Pull yourself together Anika, she heard her mother telling her and straightened her spine and looked around.

Navjyot's torch swept over the terrain ahead of them.

'What are we looking at exactly?' asked Vasu.

'That!' Navjyot said, stepping forward and shining her torch straight ahead. Before them was a wall of solid rock, mud and the odd scraggly-looking branch.

'A dead end?' said Ani.

'No!' said Navjyot.

'Are you suggesting we scale that wall?' Vasu asked.

'No! Look! Really look!' said Navjyot.

Ani trained her torch on some shrubby-looking trees. Navjyot walked up to them and pulled them apart, revealing a gaping, black hole.

'Oh! You're suggesting we walk into a giant black gaping hole on the side of a cliff? Sure why not,' said Ani sarcastically.

'I don't think that's a good idea!' Bubbles whispered, taking a step back.

Ani thought of all the movies she'd watched where bad things lay in wait for people who walked into large gaping black holes on the side of a cliff in the middle of a forest at night. Nothing good ever came of it.

'We don't know what that leads to, Navjyot,' Vasu said.

'Only one way to find out, right?' Navjyot asked.

Ani opened her mouth to suggest that they turn around and find another way in when she heard the snapping of a branch behind them.

'What was that?' she asked, her voice sounding unnaturally high-pitched.

'Probably just a weak branching falling down or something. Stop worrying so much!' said Navjyot.

As soon as Navjyot said this they heard another crack and snap behind them, accompanied by a pained grunting.

'I think there's something behind us!' Vasu sounded as though he was on the verge of tears.

'Fss! Fss! Fss! Fss!' Bubbles whispered.

'Bubbles, we're together. You only say that when we've been separated!' Ani said.

'I know, I'm just scared.'

There was another loud grunt and more heavy thudding of feet on the ground.

'Sh-should we turn around and look? Maybe we can fight it!' said Vasu.

'This is not one of your video games, Vasu!' Bubbles cried.

Whatever was behind them was getting closer and closer, crashing through the trees, its grunts and whines coming out louder and longer and angrier.

'Hurry! Hurry!' Vasu urged Ani with a slight shove. 'We have to go into the tunnel!'

'Don't push me, Vasu!' she said, stumbling into Navjyot.

'I can feel its breath on my neck!' shrieked Vasu. 'Just go go go!'

'We're all going to die in the middle of the forest!' Bubbles wailed.

'No, we aren't,' grunted Ani. 'Run!'

15

Give Me Back My Mukharochak

BUBBLES HAD ALWAYS BEEN A cautious and somewhat nervous child. His grandmother liked to tell people how even as a toddler he would look both ways before crossing over from one side of the room to another. He was wary of most new things in life, except when it came to food. So he was more than surprised to find himself running through a damp and dark and—from the smell of it—sewage tunnel with his friends trying to escape from some forest monster that sounded like it was in the kind of pain that accompanied eating one too many chicken burritos.

Was this the end? He thought of all the things he hadn't done in life. His YouTube channel hadn't hit 5000 followers, Natasha Aunty hadn't shared the recipe of her fail-proof Falooda with him yet, and he and Anthrax were just getting to know each other. Plus, he hadn't summoned the courage to tell Navjyot how much he admired, respected and liked her. Really, really liked her. Like really!

As though Anika could read all the thoughts swirling around in his mind, she reached out and held his hand comforting him just as he had tried to comfort her earlier.

'Bubbles! We're going to be okay! Look, whatever was behind us has gone! Remember, Fss! Fss! Fss! Fss!'

A scuttling sound to his right made Bubbles jump.

'What was that?' he yelled.

Vasu's torch swept along the edges and settled on a well-fed rat the size of a very large rabbit.

All of them screamed, even Navjyot, which made Bubbles feel better. The rat though seemed unfazed by their presence and sat there gnawing away at something in its hands. Bubbles leaned forward, his eyes drawn to the ochre-coloured item in its paws.

'It's my Mukharochak!' he gasped.

'Your mukha what?' asked Navjyot.

'My Mukharochak! I brought it with me to camp, and it was in the provisions room. You made us leave our other packets behind, remember?' he asked accusingly.

'That's fantastic!' said Navjyot, as the rat successfully opened the packet. Bubbles watched with mounting anger as it began to nibble his tok-jhal-mishti! The elixir that kept him going through exams.

'How is that fantastic?' he asked through gritted teeth.

'Because, it means that this tunnel leads to Sector 2. That day we found our snacks in a box marked for sending to Sector 2. If your mukhachochak made it here, then that means we're near or in Sector 2,' Navjyot explained slowly, as though he was a very small, very silly child. Bubbles made a mental note to adjust the levels of admiration he felt for her.

'Mukharochak!' Bubbles corrected her.

'That's what I said. I think we should keep moving ahead,' Navjyot said before setting off.

Ani was watching the rat in fascination. 'Do you think we should invite it to join the Forbidden Snacks Society, since it already has a forbidden snack with it?'

Bubbles had no interest in fraternising with this snack-stealing rat and stomped onwards, fighting the urge to wrestle it for his snack.

The further they went down the tunnel, the less damp and smelly it became, and up ahead Bubbles could see that the darkness was giving way to a kind of hazy light. Soon the walls on either side of them were lined with electric lights at regular intervals.

'There's a door up ahead!' Vasu had somehow ended up leading them and Navjyot had fallen to the back.

They stood in front of the metal door and Navjyot let out a little crow of victory at the sign on it, which read 'End of Sewage Tunnel 33. Entry to Sector 2'.

'Go on! Open it!' she told Vasu.

'I-is that a good idea? We don't know what's on the other side,' he said.

'Well, if you open the door, then we can find out, can't we?'

'Mi-mi-m-mi-mi-mi-mi-mi!' Vasu mocked back.

'Reeeeal mature. Fine, I'll do it!' Navjyot said and pushed down on the metal handle of the door, which gave way easily. The door swung open. It all seemed a little too easy, thought Bubbles, almost as though someone knew they were going to come here and had left the lights on and the doors unlocked.

On the other side of the door was a long corridor which they went down and followed as it turned right and then left before they arrived at the foot of a set of stairs going up and another set of double doors. On the wall next to the door was a massive map, with a helpful 'You are Here' marked with a green leaf.

Vasu read out aloud from the map.

'Conference Room.'

'Storage Facility 1.'

'Storage Facility 2.'

'K Lab 123.'

'Zepo Lab 820.'

'SB Lab 973.'

'Recreation Room'

'Gymnasium.'

'What is this place?' Ani asked. Bubbles answered her by simply pointing to the bottom left-hand corner of the map where the word 'HerbaHype' was printed. The 'p' of the HerbaHype ended in a leaf with pink and purple streaks on it, the stem of the 'p' covered in little spines.

'Hey! Doesn't that look like the plant they made us collect?' Bubbles asked, lifting the sack in his hand. In spite of being chased by some belching monster of the forest, none of them had let go of their sacks.

'Okay, now that we've *seen* Sector 2, can we go?' Vasu asked hopefully as Navjyot pushed open the double doors and walked through them. They all followed her, of course, into a large spacious lobby of sorts filled with comfortable-looking armchairs and coffee tables.

'What? We've just stumbled across what appears to be a research facility where the plant we were sent to the forest to collect is important and you want to turn around and go back? No way! I want answers!' Navjyot said.

Bubbles wished Navjyot wasn't always so enthusiastic about putting them in danger.

'I think we should put it to vote. Who wants to go back, say aye! AYE!' said Bubbles.

Vasu and Ani exchanged a look and added their own feeble ayes.

Navjyot gritted her teeth. 'You're kidding me, right?

Ani reached out a hand. 'Bubbles is right. This place is not giving me good vibes.'

'Fine! You all go back, I don't need you!' Navjyot said, shaking off her hand.

'We have to stick together!' said Vasu.

'Oh do we, Mr. Lone Wolf, who doesn't need any friends and is fine on his own? When did this change in your thinking come about?' Navjyot asked mockingly before turning on her heel and storming off

'Navjyot! Don't go!' called Ani as Vasu's face turned bright red.

'Watch me!' she tossed over her shoulder and disappeared through another set of doors. *Why are there so many doors in this place?* Bubbles wondered in irritation.

The three of them stared at each other before letting out a collective sigh of frustration.

'One for all and all for one?' Ani said weakly as they followed their friend.

This set of doors led them outside, and as they surveyed Sector 2 of HerbaHype, Bubbles was reminded of TOMBE in the way everything was laid out. But unlike TOMBE where everything was perfectly beautiful and well maintained, the hedges here were overgrown and some of the lamp posts had vines creeping up them, studded with violently purple flowers.

'Looks like no one has been here in ages,' said Bubbles.

'Hmm, I'm not so sure about that,' said Vasu. 'Look!' he added, pointing to the ground. 'These tyre tracks look pretty recent.'

They stopped at another map, which looked exactly like the ones across TOMBE. Navjyot pointed to the 'You Are Here' symbol on it. 'We aren't far from whatever K Lab 123 was. Straight down this pathway and then left.'

The squat building that housed K Lab 123 looked like a larger version of their cabins at TOMBE. The door opened easily here as well, and Bubbles once again felt a prick of unease. Who left labs unlocked? In the movies they were always filled with expensive equipment and top-secret things and guarded by killer robots.

'I don't think all of us should go in. Two of us should wait outside and stand guard,' suggested Navjyot.

'Me and Anthrax will stand guard,' Bubbles offered.

'You brought Anthrax?' Vasu gasped.

Bubbles pulled down the zipper of his hoodie to reveal Anthrax curled up and fast asleep against his chest.

'Well, we couldn't just leave her there by herself all night, could we?' Bubbles retorted.

'May I remind you that she is *my* hamster. Just because you bring her lettuce to eat, and she tolerates your presence does not mean you can just take over like this,' Vasu argued.

'But you don't take proper care of her! You left her in a vent alone! And then you were going to leave her in the cabin tonight. Alone! What if she had a nightmare and woke up? Or got lost again? Huh?' Bubbles threw back at him.

'Okay, can you two iron out custody of Anthrax later?' Ani intervened. 'We don't have a lot of time here.'

'Ani's right,' Navjyot said. 'Bubbles, you and Anthrax stand guard while we look inside.'

'If we see or hear anything, we'll use our call!' Bubbles said, zipping his hoodie back up again.

'What call?' asked Vasu.

Ani and Bubbles emitted four high-pitched 'Fss's' at the same time before collapsing into giggles.

Vasu muttered 'weirdos' under his breath as he, Navjyot and Ani went inside the building, leaving Bubbles and Anthrax alone outside. Bubbles pressed himself against the wall of the building right next to the door.

'Just you and me here I guess, huh?' he whispered looking around. He heard something creak and trembled and then began chanting the mantra his Dida had taught him: there is nothing to fear, but fear itself, there is nothing to fear, but fear itself. How long would they be inside? Maybe he shouldn't have offered to wait here alone? What if something happened and he couldn't protect Anthrax? He'd never forgive himself. What had he been thinking? He wasn't made for standing guard outside a top-secret laboratory. When the door opened Bubbles almost jumped out of his skin.

'You're going to want to see this, Bubbles, come on!' said Ani.

Inside, the lab was every bit as hi-tech as they showed secret labs in movies to be. All around them in cages were mice. Small white mice with creepy red eyes, running on little wheels, climbing up ladders and coming down slides, swinging on tiny little swings. It almost looked like they were... exercising. On another wall, the cages contained mice who were just sleeping or sitting, placidly staring out of the cages, looking zen. Or were they just dazed?

'This is so cool!' whispered Vasu as he went up to a cage and tapped at it; a zen mouse looked up and smiled at him. *Smiled.* Bubbles hadn't known mice could smile.

'This is so creepy,' said Ani.

Navjyot was studying a wall of charts and graphs that looked like the results of some kind of scientific experiment.

'The effects of microdosing BALB/c with *Luminospora aetherium*,' she read aloud. 'What's a BALB/c? And *Luminospora aetherium*?'

'BALB/c is an albino, laboratory-bred strain of the house mouse. They're the most widely used species in animal experimentation,' Anika piped up from a desk covered in folders. 'What?' she asked when she saw the surprised expressions on their faces 'Geez! Pay attention in science class, friends!'

'I guess the breach Dr. Basith was worried about were the mice. Or maybe the rats in the tunnel? She heard squeaking from the vent which alerted her to the presence of Anthrax that day. She must have thought the mice had escaped the

lab from here and entered TOMBE? And she wanted them neutralized.'

Anthrax, who had wormed her way out of Bubbles's jacket and was sitting on his shoulder, chirruped in distress. Bubbles covered her ears. 'No one is going to hurt you, don't worry!' he soothed her before tapping on one of the cages. 'These cages seem pretty secure—how would the mice escape?'

'And what does this have to do with TOMBE?' asked Ani.

'Come and look at this!' called Vasu.

They walked up to another wall covered with newspaper clippings.

Rs 140 crore funding for a miracle super drug being tested at a top-secret research facility! the headline read. Underneath was a photo of two smiling men in white lab coats with their arms around each other's shoulders.

One of them was Dr. K.K.K. Kiran.

16

Dr. Basith Is a Nepo Baby

NAVJYOT PULLED THE CLIPPING DOWN from the wall and read aloud.

'HealthUp, a private equity firm, has invested in HerbaHype, a startup that promises to revolutionize the well-being space. Headed by Dr. K.K.K. Kiran and Dr. Abram Zakaria, HerbaHype has been working on a cutting-edge, entirely natural medication for anxiety which the scientists steering the project claim has no side effects. The duo has been tight-lipped so far about the mystery drug, and insiders reveal that strict Non-Disclosure Agreements have been signed by anyone setting foot in their sprawling, heavily guarded research campus nestled in the Sahyadri Hills.'

Navjyot glanced up at the other newspaper and magazine clippings on the wall. In them, Dr. K.K.K. Kiran looked normal. His skin didn't have the plastic quality it did now and no over pumped muscles were on display. But most of all, the smile on his face seemed genuine. Not the stretched grin that seemed to be permanently plastered to his face now. She squinted at the date printed on the cover of a magazine

that showed him with his partner, Dr. Zakaria. They were holding up conical flasks with the words 'Scientists of the Year!' printed on them with a fake look of intensity on their faces.

'This magazine is from a couple of years ago,' Navjyot murmured as Vasu tried to boot up one of the computers while Ani rummaged around in a supply cupboard. Bubbles, meanwhile, was walking from cage to cage with Anthrax and waving one of her paws saying, 'Look! They're your cousins! Say hi!'

Ani walked up to Navjyot, an uneasy look on her face. 'I don't get it. Sector 2 was part of a medical research facility where Dr. Kiran and his partner were working on some kind of miracle drug. Now he's the death-defying, beefcake director of a physical and mental detox camp for tweens and teens. Why'd he move on? And what happened to the research they were doing here?'

'Look at this article!' Vasu said, holding up a copy of an old business magazine after giving up on the non-cooperative computers. He began to read aloud.

'After a dramatic—and some say acrimonious—split from his partner, Dr. K.K.K. Kiran, scientist Dr. Abram Zakaria has gone missing. His parents have filed a missing persons report at the Sivaji Nagar Police Station. When we reached out to Dr. K.K.K. Kiran with questions as to the whereabouts of his former best friend and partner, his spokesperson responded with this: "Dr. K.K.K. Kiran is saddened to hear of the disappearance of scientist Dr. Zakaria and hopes that he returns home soon to his parents and allays their fears. Members of the public who see him must approach him

with caution, due to his sensitive mental state. One cannot say what he will do. He is dangerous and bit a security guard on leaving HerbaHype." When we relayed this to Dr. Zakaria's parents they said a series of things which were unprintable.'

Navjyot watched as Vasu rifled through another pile of newspapers and pulled out one to read from it. 'Former Lead Scientist at HerbaHype discovers new calling as a wellness guru. Dr. K.K.K. Kiran, a highly respected scientist, has turned his sights from neurotransmitters to helping troubled, neurotic youth. "I've been watching the downward trend of our youth, the way they're just always on their phones, letting their brains rot, and eating junk food and letting their bodies expand. Is this what we want for the future of this country? My new wellness space, Temple of Mind and Body Excellence, will be a haven for young people who want to desperately change their ways but don't know how."'

Vasu snorted at this 'Haven! More like hell. Also, none of us desperately wanted to change anything. Our parents just wanted us out of their hair for a few weeks, and thought we'd come back as some kind of new and improved versions of ourselves.'

'Keep reading,' Navjyot prompted.

'In an unprecedented move, HerbaHype's former investor HealthUp has agreed to channel money into this venture. Their CEO, Usman Basith, cited "an alignment of core values and shared worry over the miserable state of the future of humankind." His daughter, Dr. Sonal Basith, is already a part of the HerbaHype research team.'

Ani smirked. 'Oh! So Dr. B got daddy dearest to fund her evil machinations, did she? Miserable state of the future of humankind! Who do these people think they are?'

Vasu nodded in agreement and carried on reading. 'The Temple of Mind and Body Excellence promises to use a mixture of cutting-edge data gathering and analysis, psychometric evaluations, healthy food and a reintroduction to the great outdoors as a means to get children healthier and happier. A trial run of the program is slated for the coming summer and interested parents can register on the company website.'

'Healthy food and the great outdoors! No wonder our parents sent us here. It sounds so wholesome! Who doesn't want their kids to be healthier and happier? To not be on their phones all the time?' Navjyot said, sitting down next to Vasu and looking at the photos of TOMBE that accompanied the article. 'This place looks like some dream camp!'

'Something doesn't add up, though,' Vasu said. 'This was a drug research facility. The two lead scientists were best friends. One of them goes missing. The other one opens a "wellness" camp for kids. Where they make us gather the same plant that's on the logo of the drug research facility. This lab looks like it's still functioning—someone is feeding the mice, that data over there is from last week...'

A door banged open in the distance—all four of them jumped.

'What do you think that was?' asked Bubbles, returning Anthrax to inside his jacket and zipping her in.

'It-it was probably just the wind or something!' said Vasu, trying to sound confident.

'Did you hear that?' whispered Ani as a familiar grunting sound came from somewhere nearby.

'Let's hide,' said Navjyot as she ran to the light switch panel and flipped them all down. 'Come on, quick!'

'Where?' whispered Vasu as Navjyot dropped to the floor.

'Here,' she said, curling herself into a ball under the desk. While they all huddled together and waited, Navjyot realized that their feet were poking out from the bottom, like in some bad adventure comedy movie.

Navjyot heard another angry rumble, and wrinkled her nose as it was assailed by an odour that reminded her of sweaty socks and damp woollen sweaters.

'Navjyot!' Bubbles whispered. 'I think that's the, the...'

Whatever had chased them in the forest had found its way here. A weird clopping sound, almost like a horse's, filled the room.

'It's getting closer,' Ani whispered.

'Shhhhh!' Vasu said.

Navjyot called upon all her instincts as a wrestler, waiting for the right moment to launch herself at whatever was coming for them. The second it turned into the corner where they were hiding, she rolled out and crashed into it like a bowling ball with everything she had. The monster wailed loudly and made garbled noises, as Navjyot clung to its legs. Wait, was it wearing jeans?

'Turn the lights on,' she yelled.

17

Back Stabbed and Double Crossed

'YOU'RE NOT A MONSTER!' VASU said, peering over Navjyot's shoulder.

A long groan came as a response.

For a second all he could see was hair—lots and lots of hair: bushy eyebrows, a mane of tangled, unkempt hair and a giant wizard-like beard that was not sleek and silvery but gross and knotted. Was that a cheddar Goldfish clinging to one end? A sudden bellowing sound from the door had all of them scream and jump and Vasu saw what appeared to be a white, furry camel charging towards them.

'Lulu! Wait!' the man yelled, 'Heel!'

Miraculously 'Lulu' came stumbling to a halt next to the man and reached down with her long neck and nuzzled his cheek, then bared her teeth at Navjyot, who was still sitting on top of him. Navjyot took the message and jumped off him.

'Who are you and what is that?' she asked.

The man stood and held his arms up in an 'I surrender' pose before putting an arm around whatever Lulu was.

'It's him!' said Vasu when he discerned the features beneath the facial hair 'The security guard biter! Dr. Zakaria.'

'In my defence he was trying to drag me out of my own research lab, okay? And I regret my actions deeply,' Dr. Zakaria said. 'How did you kids get in here?'

'We'll be asking the questions, okay?' Vasu said.

'Okay, but why can't I ask questions too?'

Vasu had no good answer for this. 'You can too, but we get to go first. Are you Dr. Zakaria?'

'Aren't you dead?' asked Ani.

'Do your parents know you're alive?' asked Bubbles.

'How did *you* get in here?' Navjyot wanted to know.

'Okay, one at a time. How about you all tell me your names first? That seems fair, since you know who I am and you've met Lulu,' Dr. Zakaria replied in a pleasant, non-threatening way, which Vasu was convinced was a cover for him being a whack-job-serial-killer-scientist.

'I'm Archer Babylon,' said Vasu, not wanting to give his real name.

Dr. Zakaria snorted. 'If you're Archer Babylon then I'm the Medulla Mutilator.'

Vasu felt his eyes bug out. 'You play *Brain Dead Redemption*?'

'I had an unchallenged number 1 position on the global leaderboard for three years running!' Dr. Zakaria said with a tinge of pride.

'Look, as nice as this warm, fuzzy and weird conversation is, can we please get back to the matter at hand?' Ani said

'What is this place? Why are you here when everyone thinks you're dead, and what is Lulu?'

Lulu grunted at the mention of her name. 'Lulu is a llama!' Dr. Zakaria said, stroking her hair.

'Lulu the Llama?' Vasu asked sarcastically. 'Seriously?'

'Yes,' Dr. Zakaria said. 'Do you have a problem with her name?'

Vasu realised it might be a bad idea to antagonize a possibly unhinged, known biter. So he shook his head and said no, he did not.

'Your names now, please?' asked Dr. Zakaria.

After they'd introduced themselves, Vasu brandished the cutting shears at Dr. Zakaria and asked, 'Now will you tell us what you're doing here?'

'Why don't we drop the weapons? It's making Lulu nervous.'

Vasu turned around and saw that Ani and Navjyot both were brandishing gardening implements as well, while Bubbles was holding Anthrax in both hands, arms extended as though she too was ready to attack if required.

'I am not here to hurt you,' Dr. Zakaria said. 'I promise!'

'Oh right, and all adults keep their promises, don't they?' Vasu asked sarcastically.

'Fair point. My mother told me I could have a dog if I aced my board exams and I'm still waiting,' the doctor said.

Vasu frowned at this admission. It made the doctor seem human.

'Why don't we get a snack, sit down and talk?' Dr. Zakaria asked them.

The four of them looked at each other. They *were* hungry.

'I could eat!' said Navjyot.

'You walk ahead and we'll follow you!' Vasu said as the doctor and Lulu led them out of the room down a corridor and to a door marked 'Recreation Room'.

'So, are you all staying at TOMBE?' Dr. Zakaria asked.

Navjyot grunted. 'You make it sound like it's some kind of holiday resort.'

Dr. Zakaria pushed the door and gestured for them to enter. 'Nope. You go in first!' said Ani.

'I can tell you've all watched a lot of procedural crime shows!' Dr. Zakaria chuckled.

Vasu made an annoyed face and waited till he'd stepped inside before following him.

'Oh wow!' Bubbles gasped as they all stood inside the room and looked around. The room had a foosball table, a pool table and what appeared to be a coffee machine.

Vasu spotted a bowl of fruit and rushed up to it; he'd never been happier to see a banana in his life.

'Wait!' Ani said 'Don't eat it!'

Vasu whimpered, a peeled banana halfway to his mouth. 'Why?' he cried.

'We don't know him. What if it's poisoned? What if it has sedatives? Didn't your mother ever tell you not to accept candy from strangers?' Ani asked.

'Technically, it's fruit and not candy,' said Dr. Zakaria. 'How about I eat one first, and when you see that I'm not frothing at the mouth and twitching about on the floor you can each eat one too?'

'Go on then,' said Ani, 'eat it!'

They watched, mouths salivating as the doctor peeled the banana and made a big show of biting into it and chewing and swallowing. 'Shall we give it a few minutes before we wait to see if it's laced with something?' he asked them.

'A few minutes? I can't wait that long! I'm so hungry,' Bubbles whined.

'Fine. Eat!' Ani said and for the next five minutes there were no sounds in the room except for euphoric sighs as they demolished the bananas in the bowl.

Dr. Zakaria poured them all glasses of water and then sat down.

'Okay, start talking,' said Navjyot.

'As you know, I'm Dr. Abram Zakaria and I'm a scientist. I co-founded HerbaHype—not my idea for the name, by the way—with 4K...Kiran after college. We were classmates. In college, we'd come to the Sahyadris on weekends for treks and to collect plants and herbs to test them for medicinal properties. We discovered that a plant endemic to the region. *Luminospora aetherium*—I named it, by the way—had properties that made it an excellent anti-anxiety medication. When used in the right dosage. Right after we finished our PhDs we got funded and soon we were rolling in money—literally, we did a photo shoot once where we actually rolled around in bank notes. Everything was going great.' Dr. Zakaria paused and a pained expression flitted across his face, as though he was remembering something unpleasant.

'Until?' Vasu prompted.

'Until Kiran found out that when mixed with other compounds, and with an increased concentration of

Luminospora there were certain side effects of the drug that some might think of as... good,' Dr. Zakaria said.

'Like what?' asked Ani.

'Appetite suppression leading to weight loss and a dulling of the senses that lead to a strange kind of obedience.'

'That's a weird combination,' Navjyot said.

'When Kiran found out about the weight loss angle, well, he knew we'd get even more funding for the company. Plus, he had struggled with his weight all through his childhood and teens. It took a lot of willpower and dedication for him to get fit in his twenties. So he was convinced that a drug that calmed your mind, made you open to receiving instructions with a weight-loss side effect was a wonderful thing. It took out all the things that stood in people's way to get fit. He genuinely believed that he was helping people. I didn't like any of it. I insisted that we stick to our original plan.'

By now the four of them had sat down on some stools and were listening with complete attention.

'Then what happened?' asked Bubbles.

'Kiran agreed with me in the beginning. And I trusted him. But then he went behind my back and told one of the founders of HealthUp about the possibilities. They were ready to give him an unheard-of amount of money to make the new drug. When I found out, I was furious and threatened to take the whole thing public.'

'Rookie mistake!' Vasu said.

'Yeah!' Dr. Zakaria said, smiling.

'Okay, I don't get it—why is this drug so terrible? The way you describe it, isn't Dr. Kiran right? Can't it help a lot of people?' asked Navjyot.

‘Think about it. You could give this drug to people you wanted to control and have an army of them ready to do your bidding! Imagine if you gave this to people in the army! If political parties gave this to their supporters!’ said Ani.

‘Exactly! I didn’t want my research to have that kind of legacy,’ said Dr. Zakaria.

‘How did Dr. Kiran react when you threatened him?’ asked Vasu.

‘At first, he seemed to agree with what I said. He saw my point of view. But then...’

‘Then?’ Bubbles breathed out.

‘I found out he’d been administering the drug to the other staff members and researchers here. He’d been microdosing them from the start,’ Dr. Zakaria said.

‘Wait, do you think Dr. Kiran tested the drug on himself?’ asked Vasu.

‘No, he would never do that. After all his years of feeling out of control with his weight and fitness, if there’s one thing Kiran craves now, it’s utter control. He wouldn’t hand that over to a drug.’

‘So what happened after you found out about the microdosing?’ Navjyot brought the conversation back on track.

‘Well, he locked me up here, encouraged the rumours that I’d run off somewhere, turned the labs into a skeletal research facility and converted what used to be Sector 1 of HerbaHype into TOMBE. He wanted to show investors how the drug worked, kind of like a live model of its effects.’ Dr. Zakaria winced.

‘What?’ asked Ani.

'I'm sorry, are you saying we're all guinea pigs? Lab rats? That Dr. Freakfest has been giving us this drug? Is it in the water? Our food? How?' Vasu spluttered, clutching his throat.

Dr. Zakaria sighed. 'You haven't figured it out yet? It's what they've been serving you for breakfast every day.'

Vasu thought of the green juice they'd all been drinking for the last nine days and felt ill that something so heinous had been given to them so easily.

'But why test on kids?' he asked angrily.

'Why do you think? Kids are notoriously disobedient. You don't listen to your parents or your teachers. You do what you want when you want. You're all kinds of annoying. Especially when you get to middle school. It's not your fault or anything, it's just how your brains and bodies are developing.'

'Do our parents know we're being drugged by a mad scientist?' asked Ani.

'No, I don't believe that part of TOMBE is being advertised in any of the brochures,' Dr. Zakaria said, dryly.

'But why keep you prisoner?' asked Vasu. 'Why not just...' he stopped, unable to finish the sentence. It was a rude thing to ask, even by his own standards.

'Kill you!' Bubbles finished helpfully.

'Yeah. That,' said Vasu.

'4K isn't a killer! A morally grey scientist with a troubled childhood and a slightly warped desire to live forever, sure, but not a killer!' said Dr. Zakaria.

'So you're a prisoner here?' asked Vasu. 'But you get to what, wander around with your pet llama? Also, where did she come from?'

'Oh! Lulu is from the llama farm on the property where they get the milk for TOMBE. She had some trouble getting along with the other llamas, and so they let her stay with me,' explained Dr. Zakaria.

'Why didn't you try and escape? We got in through that tunnel—didn't you know about it?' asked Bubbles.

'Look, as long as I stay inside this building, I'm fine. If I try to leave, I'm sent a small e-reminder to remain where I belong,' he added.

'Like an email?' asked Bubbles.

Dr. Zakaria lifted the cuff of his jeans an inch and revealed an ankle bracelet with a beeping red light on it.

'Like a small voltage of electricity!' Dr. Zakaria said, wincing.

'So they're tracking you?' asked Vasu in horror.

Dr. Zakaria looked uneasy. 'Yeah, and I hate to break it to you, but they're tracking you too.'

18

Capitalists Are Crazy

ANI TUGGED ON THE SMARTBAND around her wrist trying to remember what the counsellor had told her on the day they'd locked it into place.

'Your parents consented to you wearing this. It monitors your daily step count, heart rate, calories burned and sleep,' counsellor Rama had said. 'It's waterproof so you can shower with it. And let me tell you now, trying to take it off would be futile without this,' she'd added, waving a kind of digital locking device in her face.

Ani thought of how when they entered and left the cafeteria, and the data collection centre, the smartband would emit a small beeping sound. They'd been tracking them the entire time!

'You didn't think to tell us this before we all sat down for a chat?' asked Navjyot.

Dr. Zakaria had the decency to look a little ashamed as he shrugged. 'I got carried away talking to you all.'

'Are you being given the drug?' Ani asked. 'Is that why you're so remarkably well adjusted about this entire situation?'

Dr. Zakaria opened his mouth to answer, but stopped and cocked his head to the side as though listening for something. Ani heard the heavy thud of boot-clad feet come down the corridor outside the room.

'Should we hide?' Bubbles asked.

'There's really no point,' Dr. Zakaria said.

Ani tracked the ceiling for another vent covered tunnel they could maybe disappear into when the door flung open to reveal Dr. K.K.K. Kiran and Dr. Basith flanked by an entire SWAT team of counsellors.

'Welcome, young adventurers!' Dr. Kiran said as he stepped into the room with a grand sweep of his arm. 'I'm so glad to see that you've made yourselves comfortable. I trust Z here has been a good host, kept you comfortable and regaled you with stories?'

'How did you know we were here?' asked Navjyot.

'Tut, tut. Don't try and buy time with superfluous questions. You know exactly how I know you're here. And why you're here. You are here because you couldn't help yourselves. You are children with absolutely no control over your impulses, wants, needs and thoughts. You thought you had every right to go snooping and looking for Sector 2. And you did.' Dr. K.K.K. Kiran said.

Something clicked for Ani. 'Well that just proves that your stupid drug doesn't work. If it did, we would have turned into mindless zombies and done exactly what you told us to. We wouldn't have exercised free will and come here and looked around. YOU FAILED!' she ended triumphantly.

'Oh! But did I?' asked Dr. Kiran.

An alarm sounded from his phone and Ani watched as he casually dropped to the floor and began to do push-ups, like he had on that first evening at TOMBE.

'Sorry, it's time for my HIIT!' he grunted. 'Sonal, please take over.'

Ani turned to Dr. Basith. 'Your green juice was a flop! You're the C.O.W at TOMBE and you failed!'

'Oh! But did I?' Dr. Basith said as she came and stood in front of them. 'You're right, we have been giving campers at TOMBE increasing microdoses of our drug every morning in the breakfast juice.'

'Illegal!' said Vasu.

'No. Your parents signed a consent form allowing us to give you a range of health supplements through any means we deemed necessary,' she said, tossing her ponytail over her shoulder. 'But for the four of you, we've just been giving you plain old spinach juice. With no drug,' Dr. Basith said smugly.

'No, you haven't. If it was just juice, we would have been hungry as hell. Our appetites were suppressed!' Navjyot argued.

'Okay, it was spinach juice mixed with a rather large quantity of meal replacement protein powder!' admitted Dr. Basith 'We really added a lot of that! I think we stayed within the recommended limits, but who can be sure?'

No one seemed to think it was odd that Dr. K.K.K. Kiran was now doing a handstand and cycling in the air. Ani felt a strong urge to walk over and flick him with a finger so that he'd go toppling right over. 'Okay, so why didn't you give us the juice everyone else got?' she asked.

'You see when running an experiment, you need a group called a control group which does not receive a particular treatment. Control groups are a benchmark that help us compare the results of the experimental group, or the group that is being experimented on. *You* four were our control group!' Dr. Basith explained patiently.

'What made you pick us?' asked Bubbles.

'Excellent question!' said Dr. Basith, beaming. 'Do you remember the psychometric test you took at home after your parents registered you for TOMBE?'

Ani vaguely remembered an online test that had weird questions like if red is to maracas, purple is to what? And which electrical appliance do you most identify as?

'Well, it picked the four of you as perfect candidates for the control group. Discipline issues, solitary behaviour, lack of focus, obsessed with fame and glory, etc. So we decided to put you together and see what would happen. And the results speak for themselves!' she said, thrilled.

'They really do!' said Dr. Kiran, who was now moving from one end of the room to the other in a kind of strange bunny hop 'In fact, they speak so loud and clear that we've moved our investor live demo and meeting up to tomorrow morning! So they can come and see for themselves the power of our drug!'

'This is just the beginning! We have a prototype for an upgraded version of the smartbands you're all wearing that tracks your fitness levels, sends you emails and releases a microdose of our medicine into your bloodstream via the skin. Imagine corporates who want to gift this to their employees! A fit workforce that is obedient! And listens to

senior management's every command! It's the future of wearables! Schools will make them a compulsory part of the uniform and teachers will never have classroom discipline issues again!'

'You're crazy!' said Ani.

'No! We're capitalists!'

Ani noticed that Dr. Zakaria had been awfully quiet throughout this exchange.

'Don't you have anything to say about this?' she asked him.

'What can he say?' Dr. Kiran said as he walked over to his former friend and slapped him hard on the back. 'His research is the backbone of this amazing discovery that will revolutionize the field of productivity and well-being! We are going to rewire the nation's brain!'

'I'm sorry!' whispered Dr. Zakaria.

'Now, here's what's going to happen. We're going back to camp, which is getting ready for the investor's meeting and live demo. The four of you and Dr. Z will come with us. Once everything has been seen and applauded and agreed upon, we'll put the four of you into a deep meditative state with our world-class hypnotist, and you'll wake up with no memory of any of this. Or, you'll think you're chickens! It doesn't really matter! Come, B, let's go! We have to prepare for tomorrow.' And with that the two of them and their SWAT team of goons swept out of the room. Ani heard the definite click of the lock.

Ani went up to Dr. Zakaria and Bubbles joined her. 'You have to find a way to fix this!'

'I don't know how,' Dr. Zakaria said, looking up.

'You're a super smart scientist. Of course you do!' said Ani.

'Do you want to hold Anthrax while you think?' asked Bubbles.

'Umm, no, not really,' said Dr. Zakaria.

Bubbles unzipped his hoodie and took the hamster out. 'I meant this Anthrax. She's an emotional support hamster and always makes me feel better.' He handed Anthrax over to Dr. Zakaria who accepted her in his cupped hands. Ani smiled at her friend; he was always thinking of others, even while his own life collapsed spectacularly around him.

A small smile formed on the doctor's lined face.

'I do feel better!' he admitted. 'Thank you!'

'I think you have to help get things in order, okay?' said Ani.

'Right! Okay!' Dr. Zakaria said and got up, cupping Anthrax in his hands.

The four of them looked at Dr. Zakaria expectantly.

'Right! So, plan A didn't work! We need to move on to plan B!' Dr. Zakaria said.

'We didn't even have a plan A!' Ani reminded him.

'Okay, we're still going to make plan B! We're going to innovate. Do you know what the best innovations do?'

'What?'

'They disrupt!'

19

Like Steak Before a Starving Lion

NAVJYOT WATCHED DR. KIRAN AND Dr. Basith usher a group of men and women onto the amphitheatre stage with quiet fury.

After Dr. Kiran and Dr. Basith had left Sector 2 last night, the counsellors had brought the four of them and Dr. Zakaria into TOMBE. Guards had been posted outside their cabins, which Ani for some reason thought was really cool. Dr. Z had been locked in Dr. Basith's office under heavy guard.

Dr. Kiran walked towards the podium and tapped one of the mics there.

'Good evening, everyone! I'm so happy to be able to share the tremendous progress our happy campers have made in such a short period of time! It's nothing less than remarkable,' he said, turning to look at the people on the stage.

'What is it that our current workforce lacks? What are we worried about when we think of the future of work? There's a clear lack of discipline, of work ethic, of knowing that one must put in hard work. Mention seventy-hour work weeks

and suddenly everyone and their grandmother is upset saying it's modern-day slavery. Today's youngsters want time off for everything and then they complain that AI is going to come and take over their jobs. Why wouldn't it? AI doesn't get tired. AI doesn't need mental health days. AI doesn't crave sugary drinks and nachos and want to order in every meal. AI isn't doom scrolling on social media watching brainrot videos. AI does as it's told.

What we need is a way to transform today's youth into best version of themselves, with none of these addictions, cravings and distractions! And now we can! HerbaHype is here to turn slackers, rabble-rousers and never-do-wells into an army of machines. Our entirely herbal drug alters the neurochemistry of the brain to ensure that takers will be compliant and obedient, and as an added benefit, their hunger will be supressed. No more fifteen-minute chai and biscuit breaks and extended lunch hours!'

The two men and women applauded enthusiastically at this.

'Now, to show you just how far we have come, a live demonstration!' Dr. Kiran said and clapped his hands imperiously.

Navjyot watched as counsellors began wheeling large trolleys covered with silver domes onto the stage.

'Remember, friends of TOMBE, these campers have been deprived for almost ten days of all the food they loved to binge on!' Dr. Kiran said, shuddering. 'Fatty food. Fried food. Beige food! Carbs, sugars, artificial colourings. For over a week now they have been fed the food Mother Nature wants them to eat!'

'Yeah, if we were sparrows,' huffed Ani next to Navjyot.

'Let the unveiling begin!' said Dr. Kiran, and one by one, the counsellors lifted the domes off the trolleys.

'Behold, what we have placed in front of these campers!'

The trolleys were laden with food. Three-tiered cakes decorated with rosettes of chocolate. Jellies of every colour imaginable. Burgers. Pizzas.

'Is that mashed potato?' asked Bubbles, salivating.

Navjyot nodded silently.

Another trolley was brought out and when the counsellor lifted the dome, Navjyot heard a sharp intake of breath to her left from Ani.

'I-is that a...?' asked Ani.

'Roast chicken with all the trimmings? Yes,' Vasu confirmed.

Not one camper moved. They all stared at the stage with vacant eyes.

'Look at them. Study their faces. Do they look at all interested in it? They're not even looking at the food. This is the miracle of HerbaHype. It is the equivalent of placing a steak in front of a lion that's been starved for a week and have it do nothing.'

The investors scanned the amphitheatre, waiting to see what would happen.

'Camper 187, Reena Tilwani! Come to the stage, please!' called Dr. Basith.

A girl got up from the third row and walked down to the central stage.

'Reena, tell us, what do you see?' asked Dr. Basith.

'Chocolate cake and kesari bhaat, Doctor!'

'And do you want to eat it?'

'No, Doctor.'

'Are you tempted to?'

'No, Doctor!'

'Why?'

'Because sugar and fats are bad for me,' she replied in an even voice.

'And what is best for you?'

'Whatever you say is.'

Navjyot felt sick. Is this what her parents wanted from her? This kind of blind obedience?

'Camper number 365, Jerome Arulprakasam, come to the stage please!'

Navjyot watched as the boy was led by Dr. Kiran to the pasta buffet.

'What do you see in front of you?'

'Carbohydrate hell!' the boy replied.

The men and women looked impressed and whispered to each other, nodding.

'Right, I've had enough of this! Let's go!' said Navjyot.

'What are we going to do?' asked Bubbles.

'We're going to disrupt!' Navjyot said as she jogged down the stairs of the amphitheatre. 'The Forbidden Snacks Society reporting to the stage!'

Dr. Kiran laughed—actually laughed—in delight! 'I was wondering when this would happen! Thank you for not disappointing me, Navjyot. Always ready to stand up and fight! Even when you know it's a losing battle! And you've even given yourselves an adorable little name!'

He then turned to the investors and bowed dramatically.

'I present to you our control group! These campers were *not* given HerbaHype. And as you're about to see, they are as out of control now as they were on the day they arrived!'

'Out of control?' yelled Ani. 'You're the one drugging children against their will! You're the one trying to create some zombie army. But *we're* out of control?' She turned to the investors. 'You should be ashamed of yourselves. Y-you took a perfectly fine kid like Jerome who likes live streaming LEGO builds and turned him into this? For what?'

'I told you, we're capitalists! It's for the money!' Dr. Basith explained 'Don't you know what a capitalist is?'

'Why do you want people who can't think for themselves working for you?' Vasu asked the investors. 'Don't you want people who are creative and passionate?'

'They're children, they don't know what they're talking about! Look at that one over there'—Dr. Basith gestured towards Bubbles—'he looks like a small round ball. You want *that* working for you one day?' she added with a sneer. Bubbles's face crumpled at her jibe. 'If we start these children young on HerbaHype by the time they're ready for the workforce or the armed forces they won't have a single original thought in their minds! And not a single extra inch of fat on their bodies.'

'We're people. Not drones who'll do your bidding!' yelled Navjyot.

'I think you'll find that that is exactly what you all are,' said Dr. Kiran. 'You all slavishly follow social media trends. But that's okay? Doing some stupid dance challenge because everyone is? Sharing the same cat video because everyone else does? How is that original?' sneered Dr. Basith.

Navjyot felt a little uncomfortable when she thought of some of the social trends she and her cousins followed, like the time they all got bangs and curled their hair. They'd looked like poodles.

'You know, you say these things that *sound* sensible, but social media companies are run by corporations like yours! So you're *all* trying to control us! It was your slick social media feed and videos that convinced our parents to send us here!' Navjyot said.

'Well obviously, if someone is going to profit over controlling minds, I'd rather it be me than some tech bro in Palo Alto!' huffed Dr. Kiran.

'Well, you are not controlling any of our minds!' said Navjyot.

'Oh yeah?' asked Dr. Kiran.

'Yeah!' Navjyot screamed as she plunged her hand into a bowl of jelly near her, pulled out a massive glob of it and hurled it at Dr. Kiran. It landed in the middle of his white shirt with a satisfying splat.

'What are you doing?' sputtered Dr. Basith 'Did you just—' she started, but before she could finish, a clump of mashed potatoes that Bubbles had dug out of a bowl hit the side of her face. Then a bread roll whizzed past her ear.

'Whoops!' Vasu said, not looking remotely sorry.

'Come on, everyone,' Navjyot screamed, turning to the campers, 'they said don't eat the food but they didn't say anything about not throwing it! At THEM!'

'Oh, it's on,' Vasu said, grabbing a tray of mushy peas and throwing them at the investors before handing Jerome a vat of custard and motioning to him to throw it. Jerome stared at

creamy custard blankly and then looked up at Vasu and tried to hand it back to him.

As more mushy peas rained down on the investors, Navjyot and Ani went into the audience and pulled more campers towards the stage. But they all just stood there with their hands hanging limply by their sides, eyes fixed on the food but not really seeing it.

Navjyot went up to Jerome and took a spoon of custard and stuck it in his mouth.

'Can you taste that? Can you remember enjoying custard?'

Jerome swallowed the custard and then opened his mouth again, and Navjyot fed him another small spoon. He smiled this time as he tasted it.

'May I have some more, please?' he asked.

'Sure, but you can feed yourself,' Navjyot said, handing him the custard. She watched as an expression of pure delight watched across his face as he ate more. She nodded to the other campers, and he got the message, walking up to them and offering each of them spoonfuls of custard.

Meanwhile, Ani, Vasu and Bubbles were pelting whatever they could get their hands on at the adults. Dr. Kiran seemed to find this marvellous for some reason.

'Yes! Don't hold back! You're doing exactly what I want you to! Show them how bad things will be without the help of HerbaHype!'

It was the twins, Meera and Mansi, who joined in their food fight first, scooping up a giant piece of cake and impressing Navjyot with a reverse swing that landed with unerring accuracy on Dr. Kiran and Dr. Basith's heads.

'Ew!' Dr. Kiran shrieked, clutching his hair. 'I just botoxed my hair! Do you know how much that cost?' He grabbed a cup of fruit custard and chucked it at Meera who caught it and then promptly began to eat it.

'God, that tastes good!' she squealed.

The entire stage was now filled with campers who were waking up from their HerbaHype-induced stupor. Meatballs shot through the air like cannonballs. Spoons became makeshift catapults. Someone discovered that jelly cubes had amazing aerodynamic properties.

Dr. Kiran, more upset about his hair botox getting ruined, was now yelling at the counsellors to do something. And while some of them tried to stop the campers, most of them had decided they should probably just enjoy this once-in-a-lifetime buffet.

Amid the chaos, the four of them crouched behind the podium, laughing so hard they could barely breathe.

'Did you see that?' Navjyot gasped, pointing at Dr. Kiran, who was trying unsuccessfully to use a serving tray as a shield against a storm of pelting macarons.

'Epic,' Vasu agreed, peeking over the edge of the table. He ducked out and ran up to an investor who was barking orders into their phone and wrenched it out of their fingers. 'Excuse me! I need to borrow this for a second!' he said and began to record the entire thing. He paused on Dr. Basith trying to not slip and slide her way across the food-covered stage.

The chaos might have continued indefinitely if not for a surprisingly loud and firm voice.

'ENOUGH!'

Navjyot looked up. It was Bubbles, standing in the middle of the stage like an angry storm cloud. His hair was dotted with candied nuts, and he was holding what appeared to be a baguette.

The stage fell silent, except for the mulch, mulch, mulch of Dr. Basith crawling across the stage.

'Good food should never be wasted! Never! Eaaaaaat!' he yelled.

And so they did.

20

Patience Is a Virtue

DR. ABRAM ZAKARIA WATCHED AS the entire calamity unfolded on a screen in front of him and chuckled to himself. Poor Kiran had thought that watching a live stream of his moment of glory would send Abram over the edge or something. But people were so easy to fool. All you had to do was put your head in your hands and look guilty like a dog caught peeing on the living room rug, and everyone believed you were filled with remorse.

Feeding those kids his idea and then watching it all go off like clockwork had been deeply satisfying. They'd lapped up his whole 'the best idea is to disrupt' spiel and pulled it off perfectly. Perfectly!

He giggled as he watched Kiran and Sonal flail around on the stage, all their dreams crashing down around them like bowling pins. Oh revenge *was* sweet. Soon they'd be in prison, these stupid kids would all be packed up and sent home, the parents would realize there was no point suing anyone because the wheels of justice turned slowly unless greased with an adequate amount of money, and he,

Dr. Abram Zakaria, would take Kiran's measly dreams and put them into hyperdrive. He didn't need a camp or kids or counsellors or any of it. Just his darling little *Luminospora aetherium* and a whole lot of patience. And who had more patience than a man who'd been imprisoned for two years in his own former laboratory?

With Lulu by his side, Abram had plotted his former friend's downfall in meticulous detail.

It had been so easy pretending to reluctantly offer Kiran an ear for his complaints when he'd come to the lab—how Sonal was stubborn about certain things, how the counsellors didn't have high enough standards, how his LED face mask wasn't giving him the results he thought it would. And then, little by little, he'd put ideas in the other man's head: *have a control group, let me help you find the ideal candidates with a psychometric test, I have nothing else to do. Here, don't these four look like ideal control group candidates? Let's plan these games every day. Shall I help plan the menu?*

Kiran had fallen for it, and even commented many times how it was just like 'the good old days'.

The cheek! It had taken everything not to command Lulu to bite a chunk out of Kiran's back side when he'd said this.

And those kids, oh they'd played their parts perfectly. So full of righteous rage and youthful insolence. It's why he'd chosen them after all. Abram picked up Anthrax, who had been left with him for safe-keeping and stroked her little head. As though sensing that something was not okay, she struggled around, trying to free herself of his grip. Abram tightened his hold on her. He was getting fond of the little thing. As much as Lulu had been a great companion these

past two years, she had terrible breath, which was not pleasant. He decided there was no need to give Anthrax back. She was an excellent emotional support companion and he loved having her comforting little head pressed against his chest. It *did* make him feel better. Plus, she didn't kick or bite him like Lulu did sometimes.

He held her up and pressed her face close to the screen. He wasn't sure about the name Anthrax though. Maybe he'd call her Delilah. Then his two girls would be Lulu and Delulu.

'Look, Delulu! Look at the mayhem we've unleashed!'

Abram laughed maniacally as he watched one of the investors punch Kiran in the nose. Oh this was even better than the time—'OWWWWWWW!' he screamed as he felt a sharp prick on his finger. He looked down. The stupid hamster had latched her teeth around his ring finger and bitten it. Hard.

He shook his hand vigorously, but the damn thing held on fast.

She finally let go and jumped down on to the ground and squeaked before she scurried off towards another room. He'd deal with her later.

Abram sat back in the chair, and waited for the children to come, set him free and tell the world how he'd helped them, how he was innocent, how he had been wronged.

He could wait. He was a patient man, after all.

Acknowledgements

This book was made possible by Aparna Kapur because she asked me to write it and then scared me into sticking to all my deadlines. Thank you for your tenacity and the fear you strike in my heart as an editor. It means the world.

My eternal gratitude to Bijal and Sai: first readers, shoulders to cry on, and patient listeners to my kvetching about unfair deadlines (Aparna, please note), writing and other things.

And lastly, thank you to all the snacks that powered the writing of this book. I love you best of all.